I0583128

DOWN AND OUT

CAROLINE SPRINGS CHARTER

LILA ROSE

Down and Out Copyright © 2016 by Lila Rose

Hawks MC: Caroline Springs Charter: Book 3

Editing: Hot Tree Editing
Interior Design: Rogena Mitchell-Jones

All rights reserved. No part of this eBook may be used or reproduced in any written, electronic, recorded, or photocopied format without the permission from the author as allowed under the terms and conditions with which it was purchased or as strictly permitted by applicable copyright law. Any unauthorized distribution, circulation or use of this text may be a direct infringement of the author's rights, and those responsible may be liable in law accordingly. Thank you for respecting the work of this author.

Down and Out is a work of fiction. All names, characters, events and places found in this book are either from the author's imagination or used fictitiously. Any similarity to persons live or dead, actual events, locations, or organizations is entirely coincidental and not intended by the author.

Second Edition 2019
ISBN: 978-0648483540

To you, the reader, thank you for taking a chance on Down and Out.
Thank you to my loyal Hawks readers. I hope I can always bring you something you'll enjoy. xx

DIVE

Simone took my breath away the first time I laid eyes on her in the bar. I wanted nothing more than her sexy-as-hell legs wrapped around my waist and to be buried deep inside her. That night she granted me a taste. A kiss that blew my mind and nearly my load. From then on, I was addicted.

Then I went and fucked it all up when she wouldn't fall for my plays straight away. We went on a couple of dates, and my cock led my brain, not for the first time, so when she didn't put out for me after the third date, I saw it as her playing mind fucking games and considered her a tease.

Even if my brain, real brain not my knob, told me she wasn't like that, I still sought a drenched hole to sink into. When she found out, she told me to fuck off. Apparently, she'd known I was a player, so when we'd started out, she'd been giving me a chance to prove myself by dating her and staying loyal. I screwed it all up because of my dick.

When I realised I liked her a hell of a lot more than what I'd thought, it was too late. My mind seemed obsessed with her, so I let her lick her wounds for a month, and then I set out to make her mine. I had to convince her my dogging days were done.

I also prayed I could keep it in my pants until she was willing to spread her legs for me.

The only problem was I loved sex. I fucking craved it. I had to have it, if I could, for morning, lunch, and dinner. I wished the taste of pussy was on my tongue all day long. The feeling of getting off was spectacular. Hell, I looked forward to shooting my load out every time because the peaceful feeling of release was a high.

Sex was my drug, and I couldn't get enough.

How-fucking-ever, I had to be goddamn proud of myself. While I stalked Simone for a month, I managed for my hand to become best friends with my dick. Never had I used so much lube in my life because I didn't want to get rash burns from rubbing it off too many times.

Simone soon found out I was serious about her. She

couldn't *not* see it since it stared her in the face every time she turned. I'd become her stalker. Everywhere she went, I was there with a wink, a smile, and some smart-arsed comment.

It went on for a good couple of months.

After her best friend Josie went through what she did with her dad and then with Pick nearly getting killed, I thought she'd give me the chance to comfort her and, in a way, instil myself in her heart where she couldn't dislodge me. It didn't work.

It wasn't until four months before Willow showed up in my best mate's life that I finally had a breakthrough with Simone.

The day would forever be cemented in my brain because it was the day I used my best line on my woman. She was standing in line in her favourite coffee place before her classes started. She looked tired, more than usual, but still fuckin' stunning. I walked in and up behind her. When I placed my chin on her shoulder, she tensed a moment until her chest raised in a deep inhale. She relaxed immediately, leaning back into me and waited for whatever I was going to say.

It'd been like that for the last month. Her body finally craved my touch. Both her smirk and giggle told me I was wearing her down. My charm was the shit, and fina-fucking-lly, it was working.

Little did I know my next words, for some stupid

reason, would be what worked to get her back in my life and bed. I nipped at her earlobe before whispering, "If I got to my hands and knees, would you milk me like a cow?"

Her laughter was loud, free, and full of humour. She turned, wrapped her arms around my neck, and pulled me in for a dick-hardening kiss.

When she pulled back, I grinned like a fool. "If that was all it took, I would have said some other dumb shit a long time ago."

She giggled, patted my cheek, and said, "Everything you say is dumb shit. But I'm finding myself becoming addicted to it."

"Thank fuck, 'cause I've laid my best moves out just for you, woman."

She snorted. "Well, if those have been your best moves, I better show you how much I appreciate your idiocy."

I pouted and whimpered, "And *I* would appreciate you showing me just how much you adore whatever comes outta my mouth."

Her expression changed. My heart dipped when her carefree smile fled, replaced with a frown. She searched my face for something. I had no idea if she found it, but she said, "I don't just adore what comes out of your mouth, Kalen Brooks. I adore *you*. Thank you for showing me I'm worth something."

It was my turn; my smile vanished. "You always have been."

She smirked. "Just took you a while to see it."

Rolling my eyes, I then winked. "Never said I was the smartest outta the bunch."

She giggled. "Oh, I know that."

"Cheeky wench." I smacked her arse.

A throat cleared behind us. "You two going to move up and order, or stay in everyone's way and keep making us sick?"

Tensing, I looked over my shoulder and glared. "I'll do whatever the fuck I want since I got my woman back in my life. Just because you ain't gettin' any, don't be a dick about it."

The dude's hands came up in front of him. His eyes widened. "All good, keep doing what you're doing."

"I will," I snarled.

"I can't," Simone said. I looked to her as her lips touched mine, and then she stepped back. "I have to get to class anyway. You go, and I'll see you later."

Raising a brow, I asked, "My place? I'll cook."

Her little chuckle was sweet and caused my dick to grow harder. "How about I bring takeaway? I've heard about your cooking. I don't want food poisoning."

Hell, fuck Pick for catching me throwing my guts up after I ate bad shellfish. The bastard was quick to tell everyone and no doubt, his woman told Simone.

"As long as you come, I don't give a fuck what we eat."

She grinned cheekily. "Oh, I do hope to come."

Groaning, I kissed her hard once and walked out before I had my pants down trying to stick my dick in her in any way I could.

As I left the café, I seemed to have a new spring in my step. Fuck, if that was what being in love was about, I was all for it. Shit, I couldn't stop smiling like a tool. But hell, if anyone said anything, I'd tell them where to go.

I was happy.

Finally, fucking happy.

Since it was my day off, from there, I went straight home to clean the pigsty.

The garage Hawks owned off the compound was busy. Even though Pick and Billy had finally started after Josie's shit had gone down, it was still bustling with customers, new and old. Which explained why my house was filthy.

At around seven, Simone turned up with pizza. It was great to see her in my house, making herself at home because one day, I could see her moving in and all her girl shit laying around.

After we had eaten, we sat our arses down in the living room. I didn't have much in the house. It was a true man's place. It included the main things I needed: a TV, a couch, a bed, and a bathroom. But Simone didn't seem to care; she curled up beside me while we watched random stuff on the TV in between talking.

"You're staying the night," I ordered.

"Sounds like the perfect plan." She grinned.

For five months, things were fucking amazing.

We were in love.

We told each other that every night when she'd come by to stay.

Only time wasn't on our side. She was busy with uni, and I was busy with work. We were both tired, but every night she stayed, I made sure my woman knew how I felt about her.

Five months, I had her in my life before it went to shit. I'd known something was wrong when she hadn't wanted to tell anyone about us. No one knew of our relationship. She wanted to keep it a secret to see how things went. I understood because I'd been the one to fuck it up the first time. Still, she knew I was all in, but it appeared she wasn't for some reason.

It was a month after Willow turned up, and her thing with Dodge went down that shit changed. I was sure when Willow moved in, she knew someone was sneaking into the house and my bed. Fuck, it made me feel like a cheap whore, but I did it for Simone. I kept our relationship a secret for her, and then I got nothing. One night she didn't show, and I didn't know what had happened. If I'd done something.

I tried to fight for my woman. I rang her. I went to her place. I asked Josie; she didn't have a clue. I asked Nary, who'd moved in with her, but none of them knew what was going on. She'd been spending more time with her family than at the house with Nary. In the end, she even avoided Josie.

It went on for five months.

And then my life, my heart, every-fucking-thing went down the drain.

DIVE

My head was under the hood of a car in the Hawks garage when my phone rang. I ignored it and kept doing what I was doing, thinking they could leave a message because the client was going to be back later that day to pick up the piece-of-shit car. Then my thoughts drifted over to hurting Willow for even booking the car in the first place. However, she was a sucker for a sad case, and the old woman had talked Willow into taking her shit car in for a service. It needed more than a service; it needed to be put down.

My phone rang again.

Then again.

And again.

"Fuck," I cursed, wiping my hands on the rag from my back pocket as my heart took off in my chest. Hell, I probably should have answered it anyway in case it had something to do with the fuckhead Baxter, but all my brothers were at the garage working alongside me, so nothing bad could have happened.

My heart slowed.

Just as it started ringing again, I answered with, "Yo."

"Josie, no," Simone yelled in the background. Again, my heart sped up as I tensed, my jaw clenching in worry.

"Josie, what's goin' on?" I clipped roughly. Both Pick and Billy, Josie's men, stopped what they were doing and came towards me.

"Dive, y-you need to come to Simone's place, right now. She has something to tell you." Her voice was soft and quivered at the end.

Christ. If someone had hurt Simone, I'd stab the fucker.

"I'm there," I bit out, hung up, and thrust my phone in my back pocket of my jeans. Looking to the waiting men, I said, "Josie's fine, but she wants me to get to Simone's."

"We're comin', just in case," Pick said, throwing his cleaning rag to the bench next to him. I knew not to argue with him or even Billy when it came to Josie.

We made our way out the front after letting Dodge know we were taking off. He nearly bitched that all of us couldn't go until I told him about the phone call. Instead, he nodded. Concern filled his eyes before he said gruffly, "Call if you need me."

We straddled our bikes, and they roared to life. The ride seemed to take longer than it usually would. My hands sweated the whole way; my heart thumped hard in my chest, and my teeth fucking hurt from clenching them along the way while I agonised over what in the hell could have happened. Finally, we pulled up to a stop out the front of Simone's apartment building. We were all off at the same time, and swiftly, we made our way in and up to the second floor. Just as I was about to bang on her door, it swung open. Josie stepped out, her eyes red from crying. Stepping right up to Pick, she buried her head into his chest as Billy stepped up behind her, his body stiff, and his eyes hard with unease.

"What the fuck is going on?" I growled.

"Dive?" Simone called from inside.

Josie turned her face to me and smiled sadly. That was when I knew it was something bad. She reached out her hand and gripped my wrist, giving it a squeeze. "Go easy on her," Josie pleaded.

With a stiff nod, I shook off her hold and stepped into the living room. Billy closed the door after me, leaving them on the other side. It was then Simone walked in from the kitchen. With red-rimmed eyes, she offered me a small, shy smile. I gave her a chin lift, and that was when I looked down.

My eyes widened, and my jaw popped open. Shock froze me in place. "You're knocked up." Her stomach was huge, and she waddled as she took the last steps to the couch. Slowly, she lowered herself backwards and sat.

"Before you ask, you're the father." She cringed as my eyes darkened on her to a glare.

My body liquefied. Clenching my hands, my knees wobbled until I steadied myself. Anger flared inside of me instead. "And you chose to tell me like this?" I seethed through clenched teeth.

She looked to her stomach and rubbed a hand over it. "I'm sorry, Kalen."

My hands gripped my hair where I tugged on it. Then I threw my hands up in the air. I was pissed. I was fucking frustrated. None of it made sense. "Why did you disappear? Why would you do this to me when this is my kid? I could have been there for you through this. I could have helped you, supported you. But you ran, and it's never made sense because you knew I loved you. You knew I wanted us for-fuckin'-ever. Why in the fuck did you run?"

Tears ran freely from her eyes while her bottom lip trembled, and I realised I hadn't listened to Josie and gone easy on her. How could I, when I'd just found out I was going to be a father from a woman so selfish, she'd cut me out of the first part of everything there was to experience? How could I when the woman I loved shut me out, cut me off, and had just shit down my throat?

"Would I be here if it weren't for Josie?"

She wiped her face and shook her head. "No."

Pain threatened to weigh me down. My stomach flipped and then dropped in misery. Gutted. I was absolutely gutted. "Why?"

She shrugged. "I didn't think you would want it."

I picked up the picture frame next to me and threw it to the wall. My hands then landed on my hips so I wouldn't grab anything else. She jumped when I roared, "How could you think that when I loved you with everything I have?"

The door behind me crashed open. "Brother?" Billy said.

"I'm fine," I snarled. "It's fine. Everything is *fucking* fine."

As I went to walk out the door in need to calm the hell down, Simone's pain-filled voice called, "Kalen, please. Please, I'm so sorry. I know I went about this the wrong way. But I promise I thought I was doing it to save you." Spinning to her, I watched her struggle to stand. It was hard not to go to her and help. I still loved her, which was why her deceit was harder to take. We'd made a child together, something so precious, but she threw away my feelings. I didn't count at all to her in this situation.

Anger at her selfishness caused me to clamp my teeth together.

Of course I would have wanted to know. I'd want to be there every step of the way. I'd missed out on so much already: the first time she got to hear the heartbeat, the first picture of our child, the growth. Fuck, everything. I would have taken care of her. I would have helped. But I had no choice given to me and not only did it piss me way the fuck off, but it felt like my heart had been sliced open.

Her cry of pain brought my attention back to her, just as a puddle of wetness pooled down her legs to the floor.

"Shit," Billy bit out. "Josie," he yelled.

Pick was the first in the room. When Josie got through the door, I heard her gasp.

"No, no, no. It's too soon. Call an ambulance," Josie ordered as she ran to Simone's side. "Dive, get your arse over here and help her." My body jolted and my eyes went to Simone. Panic held her eyes wide and kept me captive.

Moving to her side, I gripped her arm and slid my other arm behind her back. "Come on, baby. Let's get you outside." All anger fled seeing Simone scared.

"Dive," she whispered. Her nails bit into my arm as a contraction had her crying out again. Once it settled, she said, in a scared, soft voice, "It's too soon. He shouldn't be coming now. I don't want to…."

"The doctors will get it all sorted, baby. Could be,"—fuck, I didn't have a clue—"I don't know, a false alarm or something."

We started for the door when I heard Josie whisper, "Did you tell him?" Her voice was tight with sorrow. Simone shook her head, and Josie sighed. Her eyes met mine over Simone's head, and all I saw was pain.

What wasn't Simone telling me?

We'd made it down the stairs before another contraction nearly took her to the ground. The pain was obvious on her scrunched-up features, and I wished I could take it away from her. Even though she'd fucked up big time, my feelings never vanished. Hell, I even kept my dick in my pants since she'd been out of my life, in the hope she'd come back. Now I wouldn't leave her with a choice; she was having our kid. She was mine, and she'd better bloody accept it.

Billy stood out on the street ready to flag down the ambo. I was leaning against my ride with Simone between my legs leaning against me. Josie paced in front of us while Pick stood back watching his woman, his body tense. All of us wore a frown of worry, our brows drawn down in concern, and I knew I wasn't the only one feeling anxious, wishing help would hurry the hell up. Simone looked weak and tired. She'd lost weight even though she was pregnant. It was as if dark circles had been drawn under her eyes. Pale skin replaced what used to be a healthy glow, and she had no strength as she leaned against me. Her head rested in the crook of my neck until another contraction took hold. I grabbed her and held her up as she breathed through it, but every one she had seemed to drain her each time. More worry burned low in my belly as her panting breath worsened. Her eyes drooped lower and her cheeks seemed hollowed.

Thank fuck the sirens sounded off in the distance. It wouldn't be long until we had her at the hospital, and they'd be able to help her where I couldn't.

"They're coming, baby," I said and kissed her forehead. "We'll be okay."

"Dive," Simone whispered, her voice trembling.

"They're here," Billy announced. My shoulders sagged in relief. I gently guided Simone to stand and stood behind her as they pulled up. One woman and a guy jumped out of the vehicle and ran our way.

"What do we have here?" the woman asked.

"What in the fuck do you think?" I clipped out harshly. Did she know how to do her job?

"Casey," the guy ambo said. I watched the woman catch his eyes, and then he flicked his gaze to our Harleys. She stiffened and walked back to the ambulance to grab out the gurney and wheeled it over.

"Dive, let them get Simone to the hospital," Josie said in a soothing voice. "They know what they're doing."

Glaring at them, I said, "I'm going with her."

"No," Simone yelled.

"Don't start, woman," I barked down at her as they helped her lay on the mattress.

"Please, I need you to bring my car. The keys are inside, and I'll need the car seat."

"Billy can take care of it," I ground the words out through clenched teeth.

"Dive," Josie started, laying her hand on my arm. "I'll go with her. We know you won't be far behind, and I promise I won't let anything happen to her."

Fuck. I didn't want to leave her, and I didn't understand why she wanted me out of her hair for the ride there. None of it made sense. Though I didn't want Simone worked up more than she was. Time was taking a toll on her. Finally, I nodded, and they bolted, with my woman on the gurney, to the ambulance. Before they were ready to take off, I ran to Simone's apartment, grabbed her keys, and tailed it to her car. Pick and Billy were already on their rides. I knew they'd follow me the whole way there.

In the rear-view mirror, I saw Nary pull up out front. Billy stayed back to let Nary know what was going down. Betrayal clawed at my chest. Had she known Simone was pregnant with my kid and didn't tell me? Hell, I hoped not. I was ropable already, and I didn't want to take it out on Nary. She had enough going on.

My hands gripped the steering wheel tightly as I looked in the back seat at the small car seat strapped in. Christ, I was going to be a father. Me, a dad. My mind struggled to comprehend it. Also, a deep-rooted dread pounded through my veins; Simone was holding something back from me.

Was something wrong with our kid?

My chest ached at the thought.

Pulling up out the front of emergency, I jumped out and bolted for the doors. Pick was hot on my heels. As soon as the doors opened, I was at the counter demanding to be let through for my woman.

From there, everything went fast. Too fucking fast.

A nurse led me through to Simone's room. Josie was in there holding her hand. Two different doctors were rushing around hooking my woman up to machines while a nurse was between her legs checking out something down there.

"Everything all right?" I asked. All movement ceased for a second to take me in. Then the doctors looked at the nurse.

She sighed and nodded. "All looks good for the child. It's a bit early, but we'll take care of everything."

I gave her a chin lift as another nurse came in with some space-looking crib thingy. She smiled at me and said, "It's an incubator. Your child will have to stay in here for a little while until it's ready to go home."

Grunting out a reply, I then asked, "So, the kid is coming?" My head spun. Everything was happening so fast.

She smiled, but it was sad. "Yes, your child has had enough of waiting. It wants to come and now."

My feet took me to my woman's side before I even registered I'd moved. Josie, who stood on the other side, was crying. My knuckles were white with how hard my hands clenched at my sides. Something was going on I didn't know about. But just as I was about to demand answers, another contraction hit Simone. Her eyes closed. Her mouth pinched tightly, and she bared down.

My gut dropped at the sight of Simone in pain. I'd do anything to take it from her. *Fuck.* I ran a hand through my hair in frustration.

"Should she be pushing?" Josie asked in an alarmingly high voice. Panic reared inside of me.

A doctor pushed me aside and barked down at Simone, "No pushing, Simone. Please just let us do a C-section."

What in the fuck is goin' on?

She shook her head and licked her dry, cracked lips. "T-there's no point. We all know this." She opened her eyes and called, "Dive."

The doctor stepped back, his face solemn, his eyes sad.

I stepped up, my mouth dipping down with worry. "Baby, what's going on?" I pleaded.

"G-get Pick or Billy in here for Josie, please."

My head jerked back. "Why?"

"No one else can come in. The room is already too full." The other doctor said before he stepped up to Josie's side and held his stethoscope to Simone's chest, listening to her heart.

Simone snorted. "What's one more, Doc?"

"Simone." The doctor sighed and shook his head.

"Please," she begged. "They'll need him."

"Who will need who?" I asked, confused at fuck.

My eyes stayed on my woman, even as Josie bent low and whispered something to her. I didn't see anyone leave the room, but I noticed when Pick came in. He immediately stood behind his woman.

Flexing my clenched jaw, I welcomed the grind of pain and the distraction it offered. The nurses and doctors busied themselves around the room while Josie stood and held Simone's hand tightly, but she curled her body into Pick. He wound his arms around her as her body shook with sobs.

Simone's hand in mine tightened, only just a little; her strength wasn't there. My eyes went back down to her. She smiled up at me, but I could see the strain on her face. She cleared her throat. "I'm so sorry." Tears fell from her eyes. "I love you. I always have, but I wanted to protect you from this and leave you with something to remember me by."

Fear gripped my heart and squeezed. "Wait, what? Baby, what do you mean? What are you talking about?"

Her chest heaved with a heavy breath; she opened her mouth to answer, but then her eyes widened, and her hand went slack. The machines went crazy, and Josie screamed, as I watched Simone smile before her eyes closed.

No. Christ, please no.

Cold. I was so fucking cold as I watched on powerless. My whole body shivered, my stomach churning at the sight of my woman lying motionless on the bed.

"Do something," I yelled, my voice thick with misery.

Doctors barked orders I didn't listen to. Pick pulled Josie back to let the doctors work while I leaned down and whispered, "Don't you die on me, baby. Don't leave me. Our kid needs you, needs his mother. And I need my woman. My life. Don't leave me, baby." My voice quivered. *Fuck. Fuck.* "Please," I begged her.

Her body jolted. I looked down to see a doctor slice open my woman's stomach. Seconds ticked by before I saw a baby pulled free. It was tiny, still and silent.

Fuck. Jesus, no, no, no.

I closed my eyes tight. I didn't want to see; all of it was fucking agony laced with more heartache.

"Sir," a nurse beside me murmured.

Ignoring her, I opened my eyes to Simone. It couldn't be over. Gripping my hair, I shook my head. I wanted to tear my fuckin' hair out, slit my wrists, or have someone beat me senseless so I didn't feel. I didn't want to feel. It hurt too much. Though, my body seemed to be already going through the process. A stabbing pain ripped through my chest, my stomach convulsing in agony. Still, my head, my mind wouldn't let it be the end, wouldn't accept it. "No," I whispered through clenched teeth.

People around me yelled and moved. They'd left Simone to work on the baby.

"She's gone. I'm sorry." The nurse touched my arm. I shook her off and pressed my forehead against my woman's.

"Please, come back to me, baby." My breath hitched. "Please."

"I'm sorry," the nurse said again.

My hand went to Simone's face, but it was cold. She was cold and still. No life left inside of her. My woman was gone. No longer would I see her smile, hear her laugh and feel her at my side.

Standing, I threw my head back and screamed my anguish, "No!" Tilting my head down, my eyes landed on the nurse, and I ordered with a snarl, "Work on her. Make her live." I grabbed her arm and pulled her closer. "Fucking help her."

"Brother," Pick said, his usually hard voice was soft.

He grabbed my wrist. "Let the nurse go."

"She needs to help my woman," I demanded, my eyes hard on my brother.

"Brother," he whispered, his eyes heavy with sorrow. "She's gone."

My eyes narrowed even more. "She's not."

Don't make it real. Don't take my life away from me. We can make us work. We're a family.

But they were so still. They weren't moving. My woman. My child. Unmoving and no breath in their bodies.

My chest heaved to fight for air.

"She is," Pick murmured.

He dropped my wrist when I let go of the nurse, who immediately stepped back. It was just as well because the next thing I grabbed was a stand. I picked it up and crashed it to the floor, over and over, screaming and cursing through the pain ripping into me. Through the reality crashing into my soul.

"Get him out," someone barked.

A hand wrapped around my throat, and I was pushed up and then out of the room, stumbling until my back was forced up against a wall with Pick in my face snapping, "Enough."

"Fuck you," I snarled. "Fuck you," I roared.

Ruckus arose around us. People yelled, ran, and things fell to the ground.

"I'm sorry," Pick offered.

Leaning forward, his hand tightened on my throat as Billy showed at his side, "Fuck. You," I growled. Anger was good. Better than sorrow.

Pick shook his head sadly. "She's gone, brother. Let it sink in. Take it on board and come back to the now because you need to fight for your kid."

"No." I shook my head, my eyes closing. "It wasn't moving. It wasn't crying. They fuckin' cry when they come out. It's… Fuck. Fuck me, motherfucking hell."

"It's not the end, brother. They're still in there fighting for him. You need to as well."

Unmanageable pain nearly took me to my knees, but Pick had me. He dropped his hand from my throat and held my chest against the wall.

"Fight for him," Pick whispered.

"She's gone." Despair formed inside of me.

"She is." Pick nodded.

"She's gone," I cried, opening my eyes as tears filled them.

"She has."

"Brother." Pain weaved itself through that one word, desperate and with no chance of ever dulling. I banged my head back into the wall and snapped my eyes closed. I let it all seep in. The loss, the pain, the anguish.

I let it all in until I heard a baby's cry from the other room.

CHAPTER TWO

DIVE

Dead. I was dead on the inside. All that kept me going was seeing Simone's eyes in our child's. Hours after our son was brought back to life, I found out exactly what Simone had kept from me. Not only did she have a tumour surrounding her heart, but also one in her brain. Both were inoperable.

My woman had known she was dying a long time ago. Josie told me she only found out before she called me. Simone had told her that as soon as the doctors had explained she was dying, she'd stopped taking her birth control pills. She knew she didn't have long to live, and she wanted to leave a piece of herself behind on earth. I wasn't sure she was fully aware of the choices she'd made. Maybe with everything she was going through, her thoughts and ideas were scrambled in her emotional state. She also didn't want me to see her fade at the rapid pace she was. Which was why she disappeared. All of it... everything she'd chosen to do was all wrong and selfish in a way. She'd been staying with her parents; they helped her through everything when I wished it had been me.

I wished every-fucking-day I had more time with her.

Nary had come up to me after the funeral saying she was sorry for not taking more notice, but I knew both her and Josie had been busy with their own classes and lives.

I was a dad.

A father to a little boy and I didn't have a goddamn clue what to do.

Two weeks had passed, and I was at the hospital once again sitting beside my son's incubator in the NICU area where he was still hooked up to machines. He was still tiny and weak, but getting better as each day passed. They said in only days he'd be taken off the machines, and I fucking couldn't wait for it. Couldn't wait to hold him in my arms. He was a survivor, and I believed Simone had a part in his survival. She looked over him that dark day.

A part of me wished it had been me to die. Simone should have been the one sitting where I was, talking to him, reading to him, and even singing to him in her off-key voice.

But I couldn't hold a grudge against the little guy because of it. Simone was sick. There was no way she could have lived through the strain of the birth. Even if she hadn't have given birth, the doctors later explained she hadn't long to live. She put all her energy, time, and love into our child, so I would do the same, and I'd make sure he knew his mother loved him so fucking much.

In this new phase of my life, the old me was gone. It left with my woman that same day. I was colder to all, except my son. A smile only lit my face when my boy opened his eyes. No laugh fell from my lips except for when I learned how to change a diaper the first time. There wasn't time to joke; all my time was for my son and no one else.

It was the way it was supposed to be.

He was all I had.

So I'd be there for him.

The door to the room opened and in walked Simone's parents. They visited every second day. When they saw me, a small pity-filled smile played on their lips. They were rich pricks. I'd hated them when they'd kicked Simone out a long time ago, but, in my eyes, they'd redeemed themselves when they took her in and cared for her. Showed her the love they always should have and made sure she was happy in her last days.

"Kalen," Penny said, her hand going to my shoulder. They both refused to call me Dive. They didn't want their grandchild to have a biker daddy, but they soon got over it when they saw how I was with my son. Still, to them, I'd never be Dive, especially when Simone had always called me by Kalen to them. "How is he today?" Penny asked, giving my shoulder a squeeze.

"Better. Gettin' stronger every day."

"That's great." Frank nodded, his smile widening. "Have you chosen a name yet?"

Snorting, because there was no way I was going to call my son Frank junior like Frank wanted me to, I nodded and said, "Yeah, I have."

Penny sighed. "Are you going to share it with us?"

Looking from her to Frank, I announced, "His name's Koda Brooks." Koda was short for Simone's middle name Dakoda. I wanted our son to not only remember his mum in memories, but in a way he would never forget who she was, and I'd make sure he knew where his name came from.

Both Penny and Frank's eyes teared while smiling down at me. Then Penny took a handkerchief out of her jacket pocket and dabbed her eyes. "Simone would love that."

With a stiff nod, I stated, "Good." After a deep breath, I added, "I have to talk to the both of you about something." Standing, I gestured for Penny to sit. She did, and immediately, she slipped her hand into the opening, reaching out to hold Koda's hand. I started pacing back and forth, worried about my decision but knew in my heart it would be for the best.

"Son, you can tell us anything. You know this."

Stopping, I faced them. "I need to get away. Once Koda is healthy, I'm moving to Halls Gap. My mum lives up there. She's willing to help." Penny went to say something, but I held up my hand. "I know you're both more than willing to help out, but I need to do this first month or so on my own. He's my son. I need to learn to take care of him, see where we both fit. I'm not saying I don't want either of you in his life. You can come see him anytime you want. Seriously, anytime." I ran a hand over my face and admitted, "This area brings back too many memories. Fuckin' great memories, but I want to… no, I need a change of scenery. Fresh start, for the both of us."

"Kalen." Penny smiled sadly. "We can understand it. We already do. We both appreciate how you've accepted us in his life, so whatever you need to do, we will stand by you."

Looking to Frank, he nodded and said, "It's not that far anyway."

My whole body sagged with relief until I heard a gruff voice behind me say, "When were you thinking of telling me, *brother*?"

Turning, I found Dodge and Willow standing there.

Willow reached out to her man, but he shrugged her off and stalked out of the room.

Shit.

Glancing over my shoulder, I waited for Penny's nod before following him. Willow gave me an encouraging smile as I passed, and then I heard her say, "Let me see that bundle of cuteness."

She and Josie had been a huge help in the last three weeks. They took turns to visit me, offering breaks while I showered, and they spoilt Koda with all the things they bought him. Hell, so many had offered their help, even Wildcat and her posse from Ballarat, but I knocked them back. It wasn't that I didn't appreciate their support. I just wondered if they were scared, I couldn't handle the responsibility of a newborn baby. Still, it was what I wanted to do, and I'd fucking managed well so far.

"Dodge," I called out as soon as I was in the hallway. He was halfway down when he stopped but didn't turn to face me. Slowly, I made my way to his side. He turned his head and glared at me. "You were my next call. It just happened Simone's parents visited when they did."

"Why would you want to leave when you have so much support here?" he demanded.

Closing my eyes, I sighed. Opening them, I met his hard stare with my weary one. "Too many memories here, brother. It was a fuckin' hard choice to make. Shit, I'll miss your ugly mug." He snorted. "But I want it just me and Koda for a while. It's all happened so fast. Christ, I'm not even sure if it's all sunk in. You never know, I could move and freak out when it's just me and the kid, but I want to give the two of us a chance to bond."

"You been reading parenting books again?" He smirked.

Rolling my eyes, I gave him the finger. The dick knew me too well because I had been reading parenting books. "It just feels right"—I thumped my chest with my fist—"in here."

"Fuck," he cursed and ran a hand through his hair. "You and your mum drive each other crazy. You sure you'll survive?" It was then I knew he'd accepted it.

"I think I will. But you know I'll miss your arse, so you'd better come visit with Willow and the kids."

Dodge gripped the back of my neck, pulled me to him, and slapped my shoulder a few times before stepping away. "You couldn't hold me back, brother."

"Good."

TWO WEEKS LATER, Koda and I drove towards our new house in Halls Gap. Even though I was relieved as fuck to leave the hospital, the nurses were sad to see us go. They'd been a big help in the days before Koda was taken off the machines. I already knew how to feed him, what type of formula he needed, and how much to give him. I'd been doing it since day one through the gap in the incubator. After though, they'd taught me how to bathe him, take care of his skin, and dress him carefully. I near freaked every time he'd cry, but slowly, I gained more confidence. I just hoped it stayed that way.

When we pulled up out the front of the house, my mum was already standing there waiting with a full, wide smile on her face. She looked good for her age. Not that long ago did she turn sixty, and still she wore jeans and Bonds tees with ankle boots nearly every day.

Looking in the rear-view mirror, I said, "We're here, buddy. Time to meet your crazy nanna." Worry consumed me when I didn't see any movement coming from the car seat. I was out of the car and ripping his door open in a second, only to find him sound asleep.

Fuck. It suddenly all dawned on me. I had a child. My woman had died. I was in a new place. Without my brothers. Without their support.

With a kid.

And no Simone.

Simone, who could make me smile, make me want to laugh at the world, and make me love so hard it hurt.

Now I was hurting for a different reason.

"Sweetheart?" Mum voiced as she started for the car.

I couldn't look at her. I couldn't let her see me like this. I was a bad motherfucker and no emotion should be able to get the best of me. No emotion should have the right to control me, cripple me.

"Oh, Kalen." She tried to take me in her arms until I shoved off, holding the car door, and stepped back, again and again.

"No," I clipped out roughly.

Mum's eyes filled with tears. "You're going to be okay."

My goddamn, motherfucking bottom lip trembled. I shook my head at her over and over. "No."

"Sweetheart," her voice cracked. "You *will* be okay."

When? When would it stop hurting?

Christ. I had to be strong for our son. I had to be stone, but right then I wasn't feeling it.

Everything felt heavy, like it was all crashing down on me.

Mum stepped towards me, her arms wide. I took another step back, shaking my head, and I found myself thanking Christ the house was set in a secluded area around woods, so no one witnessed what a pansy I was being.

My knees buckled under me, and they hit the grass. My hands covered my face, and I heard my mum cry out before she rushed to me and knelt beside me. My upper body fell forward as a sob hit my throat. My hands hit the ground, and I stayed there, trying to get myself under control, but I couldn't.

"Kalen, my dear boy. You'll get through this. You will. Everything will be okay."

"Fuck, Mum. *Fuck*. I've lost her. Lost her. She'll never get the chance to see our son. She'll never get t-to hold him." My fingers dug into the grass, ripping shards into my fisted hands. "How will it be okay? She didn't deserve this."

"No, she didn't," Mum whispered.

Turning my head, I looked to Mum and said, "She'll never hold him, see him, watch him grow. It should have been me. I should have died, taken her place—"

"No!"

"Koda would be better off with Simone, not me."

"You can't say this. Don't take the guilt of Simone losing her life onto you. It's the way the world is. No one can guess when or how they'll die. I'm sure Simone is up there looking down and thinking you've done a fucking fantastic job already. She didn't just get anyone to knock her up. She chose you, Kalen, for a reason. Make her reason a good one."

Hell. I could see where Mum was coming from.

"It hurts, Mum. It fucking kills me."

"I know, my baby boy. I know, and that pain will last a long time. But you need to go with it, don't bottle that up and let it fester. Let it out, Kalen. For you and for Koda."

My son's cry from the car had me kneeling back and scrubbing a hand over my face. Mum stood beside me and held out her hand to me. I took it with a shuddering breath and stood beside her, bringing her into my arms.

"It's good to see you."

She laughed. "Let's see if you say that in a month's time."

True. Like Dodge said, we drove each other crazy, and we both knew it.

But right then, I wouldn't want to be anywhere else.

"Let me go and meet my grandbaby." She pulled back, patted my cheek, and walked to the car. Mum never made it to the hospital because she was on a cruise. She had more of a social life since my sperm-supplier died five years ago. She had a tight-knit group of friends, and they all loved going to different places. There was no way in hell I'd think about the old dudes who travelled with her as some fella she was bonking.

Fuck. I went there, and now I felt like throwing up.

Besides feeling sick and dog-tired, I had to get my boy settled in with a feed, a bath, and fuck me, a bedtime story.

Making my way to the house, following Mum and Koda, I walked in and knew straight away Mum had picked well. The three-bedroom brick home had a top-notch security system and already felt homey. One of those fake gas fires was lit in the wall and warming the living room. The place was already set up with furniture; the only change was Mum buying baby stuff for Koda's room, which was right next to mine down the narrow hall.

I walked in where she was changing his diaper and blowing raspberries on his belly while Koda looked at her like she was crazy. "Did you get those things for the drawers and doors so he won't get his fingers stuck in them? What about the electrical plugs, did you get them also?"

She looked at me and rolled her eyes. "Yes, Kalen. After the tenth text reminding me not to forget them, I got them and put them all in already." She smiled down at Koda on the change table. "Your daddy is cuckoo like cocaine. It's not like you're even crawling, and already he's overprotective."

"Jesus, Mum, do not say cocaine around my kid."

She giggled. "It's not like he understands me."

"Don't matter. Cut that shit out."

She kissed Koda's belly again, pulled back, and said, "Go have a shower, Kalen. You stink like dog shit. I'll keep him entertained until you're done."

Sighing, I shook my head but found myself smiling for once. "Thanks, Mum."

She looked over at me and smiled, her eyes warming. "Anything for my boy." Then she shrugged and added, "Unless it interrupts my sexy time with Donald."

Groaning, I ran a hand over my face. "Fucking hell, Mum," I muttered before I got out of there. First, I grabbed my bag out of the car, and then I went for a shower.

Later that night, after Mum had cooked for me and left saying she'd be back tomorrow, I sat in the living room chair with Koda in my arms. He was fighting sleep as he drank from his bottle. These moments, when every-thing was quiet and calm were something special. But it also was the time sorrow hit me hard knowing Simone missed out on it all. All I could do was pray my woman was up in heaven looking down on us seeing what I was seeing: that we'd made a perfect baby.

CHAPTER THREE

SEVEN MONTHS LATER

DIVE

I couldn't believe how fast time had flown by. Koda's excitement grew each day when he learned something new. While he wasn't at the crawling stage yet, he was sitting and investigating everything around him. Every day was precious. Every day he made me smile, laugh, and love him more. Even though sorrow still cut me deep every time Simone was on my mind, which was a lot, Koda would bring me out of the depth of darkness by laughing, smiling, or rambling on about some shit I didn't understand.

But not a day went by I didn't miss her.

"Brother, let's jet."

Looking to Dodge over my shoulder, I gave him a nod and leaned down to kiss Koda on the forehead as he sat on the floor playing. Standing, I turned to Mum, who was in the kitchen and said, "Call me, if you need anything."

She rolled her eyes. "No, Kalen. I won't call if anything happens. Don't be an idiot and go out for your guys' night without worrying. But you need to think about what I said, so talk it over with your bro there. Maybe he can talk sense into you."

Dodge snorted. "I highly doubt it, Judy. There ain't much goin' up in that head of his."

She sighed. "It's sad but true."

Throwing my hands up in the air, I barked, "Fuck off, the both of you." Then I headed for the front door with a laughing Dodge following me.

Dodge had showed yesterday with Willow while their kids were at school. He'd arrived on my ride, which I sure fucking missed, and Willow was in their four-wheel drive with Dallas sitting beside her. Dodge would never let her travel alone. Pick and Billy were riding up Dodge's Harley later, meeting us at the pub.

We climbed into my Jeep and made our way into town.

"Lucky it's only a steering wheel you got a hold of and not someone's neck," Dodge commented with a chuckle.

"Fuck, man. It's my first night goin' out without Koda. You're gonna hav'ta give me a break," I grumbled.

"I'll try, as long as you keep the calls home to a minimum of two. Any more, your arse is mine to say what I wish to."

"Screw you, dude."

He shoved my shoulder. "Come on, brother. Ease up. It's no wonder Judy called me and said you're in need of a guys' night. How tight are your panties right now?"

Sighing, I pulled into the car park off the pub and scrubbed my hand over my face after I parked. "They're so fuckin' tight I can't see straight. I worry all the time. Is Koda eating enough? Is he sleeping okay? Shit, I'm up half the night thinking he's not breathing."

"Don't you have a baby monitor?"

"Yeah, but then I worry it's stopped working."

"Koda looks like a healthy baby to me. What's got you worried? Something one of those child health nurses said?"

Shrugging, I then shook my head. "No, they've said he's at where he should be. Even though he's not crawling yet like I see other kids his age do. She said there's nothing to worry about."

"Then what is it?" Dodge asked.

Looking out the side window, I stared off into the

dark night and admitted quietly, "I worry I'll lose him."

The car was silent for a while. Dodge knew me well enough to know if I lost Koda in any way, I wouldn't come back from it.

"We'll have to make sure none of that happens." He gave me a shove. "Come on, let's go get a drink. God knows we both need one."

Walking into the pub, we grabbed a booth to the side. As soon as we sat, a waitress came up. "What can I get you two?"

"Just a couple of Coronas," Dodge answered. After she had left, he turned to me and asked, "What did Judy mean at the house?"

Leaning back in the seat, I glanced around the joint to see it wasn't that busy, before I said, "I told her I got a job landscaping. Asked her to take care of Koda during the day. My boy doesn't trust strangers, but he does his nan."

Dodge came forward, his elbows on the table, his hands in front of him. "Hang on, why in the fuck you gettin' a job in the first place. It's not like you need the money?"

Rolling my eyes, I told him, "Mum's idea. Said I needed to get outta the house more before I go insane. It's true. I float around Koda all worried and shit. I need a break, but I only trust Mum with him."

"So what's the problem?" Dodge asked as the waitress came back and sat our beers down, along with her number scribbled on a napkin. She gave me a wink before stalking away. I took up the number and crumpled it into a ball, throwing it off to the side. "She wasn't bad looking," Dodge offered with a smirk on his face.

"Not happenin'. Never fuckin' happenin'." Taking a deep breath, I answered his first question. "The problem is, Mum wants to take a trip with her friends, and she leaves in two weeks."

Dodge threw up a hand, and said, "Then don't go for the job."

"I've come to realise I need to, man. I'm becoming obsessed. If I don't do this, I'll be the hermit man not lettin' my kid outta my sight. Shit, just the other day I was looking up what it took to do home-schooling."

Dodge burst out laughing. "The beard is helping people thinkin' you're a hermit." I gave him the finger. "If your job is a part-time one, I could get Willow to come up here for Koda?"

"Nah, man. Thanks, but it's putting too many out. You can't tell me she'd come up without a guard or two since fuckface is still sniffing around. Plus, she has your two to take care of." Baxter Davis was a sick cunt. Not only did he have it out for Hawks, he was into selling women against their will. He tried it with Willow, but she escaped her cousin who was going to sell her to Baxter. Thank fuck because, no doubt, the owner Baxter would have found for Low would have been just as fucked-up as the man in charge.

"Then come back to Caroline Springs. Between all the old ladies, we can help out."

Shaking my head, I said, "Not ready for it, brother."

"Why?"

"I can't explain it, but I feel I need to stay here longer."

"Everyone's missin' ya back home."

"Aw, you wanna cuddle later?"

"Yeah, I kinda do. But only if you play with my hair while we nap."

Laughter left my throat. "Fuck, it's good to see you." Dodge and I had been lucky enough to find our places right next door to each other when we'd moved to Caroline Springs. I'd come to Hawks a year after he had, and since then, we'd been stuck like glue. Some days I was sure he wished it wasn't the case, but hell, he wasn't getting rid of me. Since being away, I'd found the phone calls hadn't been enough. It'd been too long to see his ugly mug, but he'd had shit with work happening. I'd seen Simone's parents a few times. They'd been up to visit, and Koda adored the attention from them. It was like he remembered them from the hospital or he knew somehow that they were his mum's parents.

"Same here, brother." He grinned and took a pull from his bottle while I grabbed my phone from my pocket to check if Mum had called and I'd missed it. "You wanna call her?"

A snort left me. "Nope, she'd complain about what a pussy I was being."

Dodge chuckled. "So what's the plan then, when your Mum goes?"

"She put an ad in the local paper today for a nanny. They'll probably start calling tomorrow. I'll interview them, but fuck, it's gonna be hard to trust someone new."

"Just make sure to have Koda around. Kids usually can sense shit about new people. If he doesn't like them, then they don't get the job."

"Yeah, good idea," I muttered, looking at my phone again.

The bar door opened, and everyone turned that way. Pick and Billy had arrived. Their gaze zoned in on us straight away. Without looking elsewhere, they made their way to our booth. Pick sat next to Dodge and I shifted over for Billy to sit next to me.

Both offered a smile and chin lift to me. "Good to see you, brother," Pick said, his hand reaching over the table for me to shake. As I let go, Billy placed his hand on my back and hit it twice.

"Been too long, fucker." He grinned.

"Yeah, it has, but hands off, dude. I don't want Pick beating the shit outta me," I teased. I loved giving them shit, not that they cared, and Billy's response showed that.

"Nah, brother. All good. I gave him head on the way here. He's in a mellow mood."

Choking on my sip of beer, I coughed. Pick smirked and Billy let out a full belly laugh. Shaking my head, I rasped, "Fuck, man. TMI, brother. TM-fucking-I."

"Anyway, how's Koda?" Billy asked.

"Good." I smiled. "Real good. Was worried after he was a preemie, but not a problem at all."

"That's fuckin' great, Dive. Happy for ya," Pick noted.

Nodding, I said, "Thanks."

Billy turned to Dodge and asked, "You told him yet?"

"Nope," he shot back and then took a pull on his bottle.

"What?" I asked, leaning back in the seat.

"Tomorrow, gonna have church with the rest of the crew, but wanted to let you know. We got someone on the inside of Venom again. Someone who wants a clear passage into Hawks when the time comes and someone whose dad is on the run."

Shit. The only fucker whose father was on the run was Jerimiah's, club name Fang. Switch, his dad, used to be Venom's club president until the club kicked him out, and then we'd told his woman about Switch having a taste for teenage girls. He never went home after the meeting Dodge had with him at our compound. Instead, he took off and was no doubt with Baxter.

"You trust him?"

"Yeah, Parker reassured us Fang wants out of the dirty play. Never wanted in it in the first place, but Switch wouldn't let his son slide by."

"Nary's sorta dating him," Billy said.

Fuck.

"How's Vicious takin' it?"

"Actin' like he don't give a shit. But we all know he does."

"That kid needs to pull his head outta his arse," Dodge grumbled. We all agreed. No one knew why Saxon kept his distance when he had such a boner for Nary. We knew he'd take care of her well, but he wasn't taking the chance. Fucking messed up, especially when Nary loved him like he was the last man on earth. Guess she was moving on.

"Keep me updated on all the shit," I demanded.

"'Course. You're still our third, brother." Dodge gave him a chin lift.

THE FEW BEERS I'd had the night before gave me a headache the next day. But fuck, it was worth it. Hanging with my brothers was just what I needed. It'd been a hell of a long time since I'd had the chance to sit around and just shoot the shit. Things were going well for all of them, though it took Josie a while to get back to herself after losing Simone. They'd been close, and Josie had already been through so much. It was lucky she had my brothers' love to get her back to normal, somewhat anyway. I knew she'd still be hurting on the inside.

Everyone was still keeping their ear to the ground because of Baxter Davis. The dude had a hard-on for Dodge, and Hawks in general, and wanted to fuck the club up in some way. Stupid cockmuncher was out there, and we all knew he was just waiting to make a move to fuck us over in some way. Didn't stop us seeking out our own retribution. Dodge had men searching for the fucker every day. Good we had someone on the inside of Venom again. We were sure some of the fuckers in there still listened to Baxter's whispers.

It was another reason why I felt as though I had to distance myself from my brothers, which felt like a shit move. But Koda was my main priority, and I'd make sure he wouldn't be touched from the crap going down, and if Baxter showed to my house, I'd take him out. That was also why I installed cameras outside and an alarm in every fucking corner of the property, so I knew if someone got close.

Slipping out of bed, I dressed and headed for the kitchen, knowing my son would wake soon for food and a bottle before playtime. I switched on the coffee maker and got his meal ready before my phone started ringing.

"Yo," I answered.

"Morning, my boy. I know it's early, but I've already had five calls from women about the job. I'll text you the details of their appointments, and then I'll be over after."

"Sounds good, Mum. Thanks."

"No problem and try not to scare them too much."

Chuckling, I said before I ended the call, "I'll do my best." I wasn't making any promises, though. They'd know just who they were dealing with when it came to me and my kid.

The first one showed five minutes late. Not a good sign. I'd just finished feeding Koda, and he was sitting on the floor with some toys around him when she knocked on the door. I opened it to find a woman in her forties. She had a smile on her withered face and wore a long flowing dress with a cardigan.

"Mr Brooks, I'm Zoe Smith. I'm here about the job as nanny and housekeeper."

Stepping back, I gestured for her to enter. She swept in and made a move to the couch where Koda was sitting on the floor near.

"Oh, aren't you a cutie like your daddy," she cooed. Koda took one look at her and burst out crying.

Leaving the door open, I barked, "Out."

Zoe looked up startled. "I'm sorry?"

"Out. My son doesn't like you. Means I won't either. So leave."

She huffed, stood, and glared at me as she passed. I slammed the door behind her and turned to my son, who had settled as soon as she was out of his face. "Yeah, I wasn't a fan either." He smiled and went back to playing.

The next two were just as shit as the first. Koda at least let them sit while I asked some questions. One was just a young flirt and didn't care a bit about Koda. Instead, she wanted to show me how good it'd be for me if she got the job. Fuck you very much. The other I couldn't understand properly, and she had hairy legs and underarms. I swear she was part Sasquatch. I only knew that because she was wearing a tank top and short shorts. It'd be okay if she shaved and she was twenty years younger. She was sitting close to sixty.

The next one wasn't too bad; her name was Abigail Leader. Koda even thought the thirty-something woman was okay. He didn't pull a face, cry, or scream when she got to the floor.

"Are you looking for a full-time nanny and house-keeper, Mr Brooks? The ad in the paper didn't say the hours."

Sitting on the chair near them on the floor, I said, "The hours would be while I'm at work, so eight thirty to five, Monday to Friday."

She nodded and stayed talking for another hour,

asking all the right questions, but still there was something about her I wasn't sure about. Though, it could just be me being overprotective. But I wasn't sure if I could see her day after day. I reckoned she'd get on my nerves. Not that it had anything to do with me; it was about Koda.

She left with a smile on her face, and me thinking if the last one for the day didn't work out, she'd have a trial run.

The final one arrived at five. I was in the kitchen getting Koda's dinner ready when the expected knock came to the front door. Koda had woken not long ago, so he was still in an irritable mood on the floor. Opening the door, I found myself face-to-face with a woman in her early thirties.

She shyly looked up at me and said, "Hi. My name is Philomena McAdams." She was the first to actually hold out her hand for me to shake.

I took it and told her, "Name's Kalen Brooks. Come in." Letting go of her warm hand, I moved back a step and she walked in.

"Um, most people call me Mena," she offered.

"Got it. That's Koda there. I'm just fixing his dinner before he starts making a fuss like I'm starving him."

It was strange to see her wave to my son and then say, "Hi, Koda." Whereas the others mainly talked to me and played with his toys while sitting next to him or on the couch. She glanced back to me and asked, "Do you need help with anything?"

"No, thanks. I'll only be a second. Why don't you talk to Koda for a bit?" *See if he likes you,* I thought but didn't add.

"Okay." She made her way over to Koda and sat on the floor beside him just as my phone rang.

"I've gotta get that." Waiting for her nod, I walked into the kitchen and out the side door for some privacy. Then I stopped still with my phone in hand because I realised she was the first I felt like I could leave my son alone with. After a quick phone call back to Mum, where she said she couldn't make it that night, saying a friend of hers had some crisis about her husband, I made it back into the kitchen and headed straight to the bowl with Koda's food in it. Picking up the spoon, I tested it on my tongue. It was cool enough. However, my attention was quickly diverted to the living room. Moving to the doorway, I stopped dead.

Mena was quietly reading a book to Koda and my son was sitting on her lap looking up at her.

The sight sliced pain through my heart.

This was what Simone was missing.

Fuck, it hurt.

When the book finished, Mena asked, "Did you like that?" Koda replied with some gibberish, and then she tickled him. His laughter always brought a smile to my face. She shifted, lifted her knees, and placed Koda to lean against them. Then she started singing softly about some spider and water.

"Ah." I cleared my throat. Mena looked over and grinned. "His dinner is ready."

She looked back to Koda, who was still staring at her, and she gasped. "Did you hear that? Time for some yummy food. Let's go." She stood with him in her arms and walked my way. Her brows rose. "Is everything okay?" she asked.

"Yeah, why?"

"Um." She blushed. Why, I didn't have a clue. "Because you're standing in the doorway."

"Shit, sorry." I moved aside and followed her in to see her place Koda in his high chair and strap him in. She leaned down and kissed his forehead. Unfathomable annoyance pulsed through me at the tender gesture, one that made no logical sense. The woman was puzzling to me. She seemed apprehensive around me, yet she was warm when it came to Koda, like she didn't care what I thought. But then her stiff body and wary eyes told me it was a lie.

When she turned to look at me, my sour expression caused her to move back a step. "Um, sorry. I shouldn't have done that."

With a grunt, I walked to the bench, grabbed Koda's dinner and took the seat in front of him. His eager, hungry eyes made me smile. He had his mouth open even before the spoon was near him while slapping his hands on the plastic in front of him.

"He likes that," Mena commented. Looking at her, I saw she was smiling fondly down at Koda. She glanced up and saw me looking. "Is there anything I could do? Like, make you dinner or anything? I mean, what would the job entail? I understand housework and taking care of Koda. But, um, for extra money, I could have a meal ready for you when you got home from work." She shrugged. "It was just a thought."

Raising a brow at her, I noted, "Already asking for extra money and you don't even know if you got the job."

Her cheeks shone red. "Sorry, that was rude."

"Nah, straightforward, which is what I'd want with someone around so often."

She nodded. "I could do that. Be straightforward. Starting with the fact Koda seems to eat a lot of jar food." She eyed the counter. "If I got the job, I would like the chance to make him his food as well as yours."

Was she trying to get to me through my stomach? Because dammit, it could just work. Mum wasn't much of a cook. I still ate what she made, but often I wondered how my stomach was going to cope in the long run.

"Don't you have a family to run home to?"

She looked to the floor and back up, jutting her chin out a little. "No." I could sense she wasn't willing to add more. No skin off my nose. The less I knew about the woman, the better. Though… "You got a police check, right?"

She nodded and went to her bag by the door. I hadn't even noticed her drop it in the first place. She came back talking, her eyes focused on her bag as she went through it. "I have a blue card and police check. I've never even had a parking ticket."

Placing Koda's now empty bowl on the table, I reached for the papers and looked them over. "No ex stalking you, wanting your blood for running off, or a family member wanting to sell you?" The room went silent until Koda let out a squeal. He wanted his fruit. I glanced up, my gaze landing on Mena's pale face. "What's wrong?"

"What sort of women have you been around to ask those type of questions?"

My eyes narrowed. "Good women in bad situations. If I hire you, I need to know if you're bringing a situation to my doorstep. Will you?"

"No. I, um, I have no family in this area."

After studying her, I finally deemed her words true and offered a chin lift. I put the papers on the table and grabbed a jar of fruit. Before opening it, I asked, "You gonna give me shit for feeding him this?"

"Besides the fact it's full of preservative, no." She smiled.

Shit. If she could get my son eating better and checked all the right boxes, she was the best out of the lot of them that day. None of the others gave two hoots about what Koda was eating.

"Mena," I said to grab her attention from Koda. "See you Monday at eight thirty. I start work at nine and Koda usually wakes just before then. It'll be until five from Monday to Friday."

Her hands clasped in front of her heart, and her smile grew big. "I got the job?"

"Yeah, woman. But you fuck my kid or me over, be prepared to face what happens."

She nodded. "I got you. I mean, I won't... do what you said."

Only time would tell.

CHAPTER FOUR

MENA

After leaving Mr Brooks's house, I found myself smiling with hope in my heart, which hadn't happened for a while. Excitement about the job sent a thrill throughout my body, causing me to shiver. It also made me smile giddily and want to dance because I'd get to spend a lot of my time with Koda. He was such a gorgeous little boy. Each smile, laugh, and look from him was precious. Even after such a short time with him, I knew that much already.

Not only did I feel lucky to have a job where I would spend it looking after a cute little monster, but I needed the job like I needed a new place to live. If I knew nine months ago, I would be in the spot I was, I would have done something about it. But I didn't, so there was no point in living with regrets. They got a person nowhere in life.

And that was why I didn't regret marrying my childhood friend, Mark.

It would be easy for me to do so, but again, it would get me nowhere.

Mark and I had been inseparable since kindergarten. We were there for each other in every way. He was my rock when first my mum died and then my dad. Then I had the chance to be there for him when his dad passed. Some would say we'd had a tragic life, so much death, so much misfortune, but we made sure we had each other and that was all that mattered.

It wasn't until two years earlier that Mark asked me to marry him. I knew I loved him. He was my best friend after all. Only, he loved me in a different way.

Never had I pictured us in a relationship, but I was worried I would lose him if I said no. I was worried I would lose the only person who had been there from the start.

Guilt played a big part in my life over the previous year.

I felt guilty I didn't love him like he did me.

I felt guilty for giving in and promising him a part of me that I couldn't give. My whole heart.

And guilty because of the anger I felt for him, when he was so important to me, had grown inside of me in the last year.

If I hadn't married him, I wouldn't be where I was.

Then again, I wouldn't have been able to see him before he died. I still, even after it all, cherished that morning kiss goodbye.

Six months earlier, Mark was on his way to work his night shift when there was an accident. An accident he caused because he was drunk. An accident that not only took his life, but the life of a mother. When the police came to our door the next morning, I knew something bad had happened. I'd felt it deep within me. My body stiffened only to fall to the floor in a heap while I'd burst into heaving sobs of tears. Unbearable pain had coursed through me knowing I'd never see Mark again.

He'd been drunk that morning because he'd been stressed. I blamed myself when I hadn't smelt it on him before he left. I blamed myself in many ways. We were in a lot of debt and couldn't seem to climb out. It wasn't a situation we needed to be in. However, Mark had always liked the best in life. A new apartment, a new car, a new beginning. He didn't understand I didn't need or *want* any of it. All I cared about was his happiness. Yet more guilt, when I foolishly let it happen and didn't say a thing. Since then, a pang of sorrow lived inside of me and always would because I'd lost the last person I loved in my life. However, on some days, anger would take over. Anger would rise to the surface because he'd stupidly drank that day and caused an accident taking his life, a life I'd cherished. He was my best friend, my world, my only. And because of his stupidity, he'd left me to live a life without him.

As luck would go, the day before Mark's death, I'd lost my job due to cutbacks. I'd been the last to be hired, so I was the first to go. I hadn't had the courage to tell Mark that night. His anxiety levels had already been through the roof. Then, the week that followed, I was kicked out of the house. I had to sell my car to get a cheaper one, and I found myself sleeping on the streets in my car because I had nowhere else to go, no close friends and certainly no family.

I didn't choose to be living out of my car. I'd applied for houses, but with the bad record marked against my name, it meant no one would rent to me. I had been able to claim benefits, but most of the money I received from the government was put against my debt. It was a desperate attempt to clear the negative and start fresh. What little I had left over paid for fuel and food.

I smiled. I finally had a job!

As I walked to my car from Mr Brooks's house, relief fluttered in my chest. This job was the chance I needed to get on my feet. I reached my small Tarana and glanced at all that I owned. There was no way I could let my boss know this was my sleeping arrangement. No one would want to employ someone who was homeless.

I brushed aside the thought as I pulled away. It was time to celebrate my success. Driving down the road, I planned what to eat that night. I would splurge a little. Anything would be better than two-minute noodles with the warm water from a gas station. I considered if, with my new job, I'd be able to eat there. I hadn't actually asked the rule about eating at Mr Brooks's house. Would I be allowed to feed myself during the day? God, he could want me to bring my own lunch, which I would do, but then he'd see the stale bread I ate.

I sighed and decided I'd deal with the unanswered questions on Monday. I was working myself up unnecessarily. I allowed myself to grasp on to the fact that the money I should make during the week would give me an extra $20 a week more than what I got from the government and *if* Mr Brooks didn't mind my eating their food while minding Koda, I had the chance to start saving.

By the time I'd left Mr Brooks's house, it was already six. It was time to celebrate my new job. I hadn't done anything for myself in a long time, and if I regreted it come Monday, I would deal with it then. I'd learned many times my body could go without in dire situations; it was nothing new. My excited mood, however, helped my annoying conscience to settle down as I pulled into the car park of the supermarket.

My stomach grumbled while my eyes had an orgasm over all the food. I knew as soon as I paid for the food remorse would take over, but right then, I was more than eager to grab some deliciousness. First, I went to the toiletry aisle and grabbed a fresh, cheap tube of toothpaste and some sanitary napkins. I still had enough shampoo and conditioner in the car to last me for at least two more weeks. When I could, I showered at the community showers for the homeless. However, they weren't always open, so some of the other days, I washed my hair in the gas station bathroom, or I drove to one of the local waterfalls at night when I knew no one would be around. It was cold, but it was always worth it.

When I was low on fuel, I walked everywhere I had to go, which was why I chose to sleep in the car close to the centre of town. Though, I considered changing that to park close to Mr Brooks's place so I wouldn't be late. Something told me he would hate tardiness. Actually, he seemed like the kind of man to hate a lot of things, except his son. From his gruff and glaring exterior, I knew there was a story behind it, and it wasn't hard to guess it had a lot to do with Koda's mum, whoever that was. He kind of scared me, especially when I, without thought, leaned in to kiss Koda's forehead. His scowling face looked like he considered stabbing me. I had to remember no overfondness to Koda while he was around.

My body was already weary as I made my way up to

the cash register to pay for my half-full basket. Tiredness was something I was used to. It came with sleeping in a small car and not getting enough shut-eye because all noises through the night spooked me. Ever since a drunk man stumbled across my car one night when I was asleep and started pounding on the roof, yelling, "I can see you in there. Come on, pretty, open up and I'll show you a good time." Never had I moved so fast into the front seat. I'd started the car and sped out of there. Since then, I made sure I was vigilant during the night. I didn't want anyone to accidently stumble across my path. There were many sickos out there, and I refused to be a victim. I only had myself to protect me, so I was smarter with where I parked and who I spoke to.

"Evening." The man serving me smiled. He was in his late fifties. "Nice night out there. I nodded and offered a small smile in return. It was a pleasant evening. I loved the warmer nights. It meant I wouldn't freeze in the car or have to pile clothes upon clothes on to try to stay warm. "That'll be twenty-nine, seventy."

Cringing, I looked down into my purse and grabbed out the twenty and the five-dollar note. "Um, sorry, can I take off the deli meat?" My face heated. I should have kept a better total. Then I remembered I didn't take the toiletry items into account. Foolish amateur move. My mind was too occupied.

"No worries, love. New total is twenty-four, ninety."

Handing him over the money, I waited for the change, all ten cents of it. There was no pretence in my life, and I certainly wouldn't scoff at any change I received. It would add up to something I could buy the next time.

After I made my way to my car and drove ten minutes to a secluded area I'd discovered since I arrived in Halls Gap, I parked, grabbed my grocery bag, and hopped out of the car, making my way to the back where I sat on the trunk.

Sighing, I took a moment and looked up into the black night. Stars shone, their light greeting me. The one good thing about being homeless was that I never missed seeing the stars twinkling every night and appreciating how they shone down on me. It meant there was more out there in the world, and it made me feel there was more meant for me in the world.

At least I could only hope.

My stomach once again growled in complaint. Smiling to myself, I patted my stomach and opened the grocery bag next to me. It was a hard decision, but I chose a small piece of mud cake first. The fruit and vegetables would be for later and the weekend. I'd try to make the mud cake last as well, but I had a sweet tooth, and it was something I rarely bought. Also in the grocery bag were peanut butter and bread, a necessity because bread filled my grumbly stomach.

After I'd eaten, I cleaned my teeth using the water I'd

bottled from the waterfall to rinse. In the back seat, I then dressed in track pants and a jumper, dragging blankets over me as I lay back against my pillow.

Only sleep wasn't on my mind, Koda Brooks was. I'd always wanted a baby, but my life was never financially stable to have one. I didn't want my child going without like I had with my parents. I loved my parents with my whole heart, but they were lost. Going from job to job and sometimes no job at all, we'd scraped by every week. As a child who wore thrift shop clothing, I was constantly teased at school. I would never want my child to have the life I had.

Besides, I still had time. I was only thirty. There were older women out there still having babies. All I had to do was find a stable job. After I'd made leeway with my debt, I could find a nice, caring man and hopefully, by the time I was fifty, I would have a child… because I doubted I'd have everything paid off until then.

At least for the time being, I got to spend time with such a cute little man. I smiled to myself as I lay there thinking of Koda and his squishy, pinchable face.

Monday couldn't come fast enough.

Then I sent a silent prayer to God, asking for strength when it came to Mr Brooks. He seemed like a hard man to get along with, and I knew without a doubt, the threat he made was true. If I caused any type of trouble for

Koda or him, I would regret it, and honestly, I wasn't sure if I would survive his type of payback.

A shiver raked my body thinking of his hard steel eyes.

I wondered why he was so quick to offer me the job on the spot. Could it be possible the other women were worse than what I was? I knew there were others up for an interview when Mr Brooks's mum mentioned it. She seemed like a nice woman, which left me wondering how and why he had become the opposite to her.

I guessed come Monday I would find out about him a little more.

Another shiver ran over me.

I wasn't sure I wanted to find anything out about him and his world.

CHAPTER FIVE

MENA

Early Monday morning, I found the perfect spot to store my car near my new job. Thankfully, bushland surrounded the house, so it made it easier for me to find a great hiding spot where no one would find it. The walk to the house only took twenty minutes, and it was a pleasant walk. I was glad the day was yet another sunny one. Still, the weather in Victoria was temperamental.

Taking the steps up to the front door, my heart beat faster in my chest. Nerves churned my stomach and with a trembling hand, I reached out and knocked.

"Come in," was clipped out harshly and loudly.

Opening the door, I walked in to find Mr Brooks in the kitchen with Koda already in his high chair while having some breakfast.

"Morning." I smiled. A grunt was offered from Mr Brooks and when Koda looked over to me, he smiled, warming my heart.

"Mum will be here in an hour. She'll show you through the ropes, what Koda likes and his normal sleeping time and stuff," he explained and stood from his chair, taking the bowl with him to the sink. "Not sure how Koda will go when I leave. He's used to his nanna being here, so he might make a fuss and cry when it's just the two of you."

"Don't worry, Mr Brooks. I can handle it."

He turned, his eyes hard. "You had much experience with kids?" He would have already seen my answer on my resume. Still, I humoured him.

"In my early twenties, I used to work in a child care centre. I left because I wasn't happy with the person who ran the centre. It had nothing to do with my work." Which was what he really would have wanted to know, but he seemed to like to play around it to try to intimidate me. "I know what I'm doing. I promise."

He eyed me from top to bottom. Suddenly, I felt very dirty, even though I'd washed my clothes during the weekend.

Jutting my chin out, annoyed with his appraisal, I shot out, "He will be in good care with me."

"Right. Well, cook and eat what you like." I quickly wiped my hand across my mouth to hide my wide smile. Relief swept over me. "Koda likes a bottle before his naps, both times. His formula is in the cupboard. Text me a list of what you want at the grocery store, and I'll pick it up on the way home."

Well, dang. "Um, I, ah, broke my phone recently, and I haven't had the chance to get a new one." Since six months ago.

Again, he studied me and then sighed. "I've left my number near the phone. Ring me around five and I'll get the stuff then."

"Okay."

Koda started to whine and fidget. He didn't like just sitting there. Before his dad could get to him, I walked across the room and pulled him into my arms, sitting him on my hip. "Good morning, little man." I tickled his belly. He giggled and then reached out and grabbed a fistful of my blonde shoulder-length hair, giving it a tug. Of course, he laughed more when I said, "Ouch."

"Yeah, he likes to do that," Mr Brooks said while running a hand over his chin. It seemed Koda liked his dad's beard. "Anyway, I'm gonna hit the road." He didn't move. In fact, he looked like he really didn't want to.

With a quiet, calm voice, intended to reassure him, I said, "He will be fine with me, Mr Brooks."

"Dive."

My head jerked back. "Sorry?"

"Call me Dive."

My brows dipped in confusion. I'd thought his name was Kalen. Maybe it was a nickname or something, but I wouldn't pass on the chance to call him something else than Mr Brooks.

"Um, sure. What does it mean?"

Shaking his head, he said, "It doesn't matter." He looked at his watch and cursed. "I really have to get going."

"No worries." I picked up Koda's free hand, the one not wrapped around my hair, and waved at Dive, a name I wasn't sure I would get used to. Maybe I should go back to calling him Mr Brooks. "Wave to Daddy." I smiled over at Mr Brooks and said, "Bye-bye, Daddy."

His lips twitched. He stalked our way, kissed Koda quickly on the cheek, and then started for the front door. "See ya later. Call for anything." He glanced over his shoulder. "Don't fuck me over, Mena. I won't like it."

"I won't."

"Good." He opened the front door and stepped out, slamming it behind him.

Looking down at Koda, I blew out a raspberry and said, "Wow, kiddo, that was tense." He smiled.

I jumped when the front door opened again. He went to bark out something, then stopped, and looked at his son with surprise flashing in his eyes. "He's not crying."

Glancing down at Koda, I looked back to Mr Brooks and stated, "Well, no."

He ran a hand over his face. "Where's your car?" He glared.

"Um, at home. I took the bus."

"The bus stop is a long way down the road. Don't like you walking that far. Not safe. I'll drive you to the bus stop tonight."

"No!" Blushing, I added, "I mean, I like the walk, and it's not far, honestly."

"We'll see," he grumbled and left again.

I waited to see if he was going to come back in for something else, but he didn't. So I made my way into the living room to sit with Koda on the floor.

An hour of fun with Koda went by fast, and then the front door swung open once again. "Where's my grand-baby?" A woman in her fifties, wearing jeans and a tee waltzed in. She picked Koda up and gave him a big sloppy kiss. "Hi." She smiled once I stood next to them. "You must be Philomena. I'm Judy, Kalen's mum. You know, you should really lock the front door after my son leaves. He would hate the thought of it being unlocked where anyone could walk in."

"Um, yes, okay. I'll make sure I do that and please, call

me Mena."

"Will do." She grinned and looked me up and down, much like her son had. "You're a skinny little thing, aren't you?" I had no response, so I said nothing at all. "So, how's it been with Kalen? Don't let him intimidate you. He's sweet and soft once you get to know him. Though, he probably won't let his guard down for a long time yet. Stick in there and don't take his shit, and you'll be fine."

"Ah, thank you. I'll make sure I do."

Again, she studied me. "Good." She nodded. "Now, let me show you the routine Koda and I have, but feel free to add your own in."

Smiling, I said, "Sounds like a plan."

Judy spent the morning showing me where things were around the house, all cleaning items, and Koda's clothes and how to use the washing machine. I got giddy at the thought of bringing my clothes to the house to wash. Mr Brooks would be none the wiser, so it wouldn't hurt. She instructed me with how Koda liked a nap after his bottle, which was after a book, a hug, and a fresh nappy. Once she placed him in his crib, he soon drifted off without a sound. He was such a good baby. The best I had ever met. For lunch, while Judy played with Koda after he woke, I made a dish of roasted beef and vegetables. What I didn't mulch up for Koda, Judy and I ate.

We all sat at the kitchen table enjoying the meal and

each other's company. Judy was really easy to get along with.

"How are you finding things so far?" Judy asked.

"I'm loving it." I smiled. "Koda is such a great baby. But I think he needs to start on more solid foods. He seems to get bored with the baby mash. I wondered if Mr Brooks wouldn't mind my introducing some things."

Judy started giggling. Once she calmed she said, "You call him Mr Brooks. I bet he loves that."

"Well, no. He did say to call him Dive this morning, but I can't seem to bring myself to do it."

She rolled her eyes. "That stupid name." She shook her head. "Just call him Kalen, love. I'm sure he won't say anything about it. As for solid food, I've tried in the last month to get my son to start, but he worries Koda will choke on it." She got a cunning look in her eyes. "Maybe if you start without his knowing, you can eventually show him it would be fine for Koda, and I really think Koda would love it."

Biting my bottom lip, I thought about it. "I'm not sure if I should. What happens if… Kalen doesn't like my choice, and I get fired." Looking at Koda, I whispered, "I don't want to get fired. I can't."

The silence in the room was harsh. Even Koda was quietly studying me.

A warm hand landed on mine. "You do this for Koda and let me take care of Kalen." Opening my mouth to say more, I didn't get a chance. Her hand came up in front of my face. "No, I promise, you won't lose your job for helping Koda out. Kalen will eventually see that. Don't be afraid of him, Mena. You need to stand your ground with him. Besides, I already heard you asked to be the one to cook for them both." She smiled. "Don't stress, love. He'll be fine."

She was right. I did have the lady balls to stand up to Kalen. Heck, I did it when I first met him, so what had me not wanting to with this? Maybe the scary look in his eyes?

However, Koda needed more nourishment and food that he could get excited over. Besides, it was what I was paid to be there for. Koda.

"Okay, I'll start."

"Great." She clapped.

After lunch, Judy left to let me handle the afternoon naptime. I hoped Koda would be able to go down peacefully as he had for Judy. Before his nap, though, the sunshine beckoned to me. After finding Koda's stroller and finally managing to fold it down, we were ready to head outside for some fresh air.

Koda seemed to love the walk. I told him all about the plants around us and let him feel all the leaves and pine cones. All he tried to eat, which made me laugh. After an hour of fresh air, we went back inside. I sat Koda in the high chair for an afternoon snack before I put him down.

I stood in the kitchen with my hands on my hips contemplating on whether I should try something new, just something small before his bottle. With courage, I cut up some banana and grabbed a dry cracker. I made sure I was sitting right in front of him if anything went down the wrong way. When I placed the plate in front of Koda, his eyes went wide. He slapped his hands on the plastic of the high chair and then squealed before latching onto some banana in one hand and a cracker in the other. I had to chuckle when he eyed both hands like he couldn't make up his mind on what to try first. Then he shoved a piece of banana in his mouth and chomped down.

It was a delight to see him enjoy them so much and not once did he have trouble. He sucked and dribbled all over the crackers to make them soft enough to eat.

There was a lot to clean up afterward. He seemed to have gotten it everywhere, even in his hair. His joy was worth the extra work. As he lay on his back on the change table in his room, I couldn't help but notice how much he looked like his father. The dark brown hair, the steel eyes, the cute nose, and if Kalen smiled, I imagined he would also have a dimple in one cheek.

"What happened to your momma, baby boy?"

Koda babbled something.

"No matter. I'm sure you have lots of love. I can tell your daddy loves you so much." Kissing his cheek, I placed him in his sleepsuit and read him a book while sitting in the rocking chair in the corner and feeding him his bottle. I looked down at him as he fought sleep and listened to my words. After I had sat him up, he let out a big burp. I then gave him another kiss and placed him in his crib. What I actually felt like doing was to hold him while he slept, but I thought better, knowing it would undo the good routine they had.

Leaving his door open a little, I made my way into the kitchen to tidy up, and while Koda slept for an hour and a half, it gave me time to clean the rest of the house. Which I was sure Judy had already been doing because if it had been just Kalen, a typical male, the house would have been a disaster zone. I then started on dinner. I had enough from lunch for Koda's dinner, and I decided I'd cook Kalen a steak with scallop potatoes and carrots.

CHAPTER SIX

DIVE

The day was fucking hot to be outside working my arse off in. What in the hell had I been thinking, getting a job as a landscaper? Well, not really a landscaper, but his lackey. I did all the shit jobs while the old dude got to do all the easy ones. Though, I shouldn't fucking complain. The old man did seem in his sixties. He probably needed the break, and at least it gave me a workout. I was just being a little bitch complaining because I missed Koda like crazy.

Dead on five, as I walked to my car, my phone rang. All day I thought I'd get a call saying something was wrong, but it never came. Well, besides my mum where she told me she thought Mena was amazing with Koda. Just hearing that put my heart at ease, well somewhat.

Putting the phone to my ear, I answered with, "Yo."

"Um, hi, ah Kalen. It's Mena."

"Got that, woman, when my home number showed up on the phone."

"Right." She sighed. "I have a list for you like you asked."

"Give it to me."

"Do you have a pen and paper?"

"I'll remember."

"Right," she mumbled and then rattled off about a dozen items. Fucking lucky I had a good memory. I didn't expect so much; then again, I hadn't noticed we were near out of detergent and toilet paper.

"Got it," I noted and then hung up. I felt like a cunt being short with her. But she wasn't there as a friend. She was an employee, and that was all.

After a visit to the supermarket, it was nearly dark by the time I pulled up out the front of my place. Lights shone out the windows. Fuck, I'd have to make sure she closed them as soon as it got dark. I didn't want any fucker to be able to look in the house.

Grabbing the groceries, I walked to the front door just as it opened with Mena filling it.

"Do you need a hand?" she asked with a small grin.

"Nope, got it all," I said, moving past her into the

living room. A smile lit my face seeing Koda sitting on a beanbag in front of the TV. His attention was all for some fucked-up show. Quickly, I placed the bags in the kitchen and walked back out to my boy.

Getting to the floor on my knees, I pulled the bag around to face me, and once Koda saw his daddy, he smiled, his hands reaching right out to me. He was in my arms in the next second, where I brought him close and drew in his scent.

"Hey, buddy. Missed you." His reply was to grab my beard and tug on it, causing me to chuckle. One of his fists made its way into my mouth, then out again to wipe my saliva over my face. Not the best greeting, but it would do. Anything would do when it came to Koda.

"He been good?" I asked. When I didn't get an answer, I looked over my shoulder where I expected to find Mena standing there, only she wasn't.

I stood with Koda and walked into the kitchen; she'd already put everything I brought away and something smelled fucking great. I hadn't noticed earlier; I was too keen to get to my son.

"Was he good today?" I asked again, causing Mena to jump since her head was halfway in the fridge.

She stood and spun with her hand on her chest. "Sorry?"

"I asked if Koda was good today?"

She grinned. "Yes. He was perfect. Not a problem at

all. He's already had his dinner." Then she fidgeted, so something was on her mind. I raised a brow at her. "Um," she started.

"What?" I snapped.

"No, it's nothing wrong. But, I um, I did some studying on the weekend about babies Koda's age, and it said that it would be good to start introducing solids more. I asked your mum about it. She said it was a good idea. So today, I gave him a banana and crackers just to start out, to see how he went, and Koda loved them. You should have seen his face. He was so excited, he…." She trailed off, her eyes widening at my scowl.

"Did you fuckin' think to ring me, his goddamn father, and ask me?"

She shook her head. Her eyes went to the floor. "No, sorry."

Koda started to whine in my arms, but I hadn't finished. "He could have choked. He could have been fuckin' allergic to something. You can't just do shit without me knowing, woman. You ain't his fuckin' mother."

"I would never try to be," she muttered to the floor.

"Jesus," I snarled. "The first day you come here, and already you get him outta routine. Already you don't fuckin' think about what *his* father would want."

Her chin came up and jerked out. "Am I fired?"

Glaring, I clenched my jaw so I didn't yell *yes!* "I'm

going to get Koda changed for bed." Like a dick, I gestured to the kitchen. "Tidy this shit up, and maybe do as I tell you and pay you to do." Turning, I stalked from the room.

"Wait," she called out, rushing into the living room. As I met her gaze from looking over my shoulder, she asked again, "Am I fired?"

"No," I snapped.

"Okay." She sighed. I saw her shoulders relax, and tension leave her body. Only I didn't say anything else. I walked to Koda's room.

By the time I finished putting Koda to bed and came out into the kitchen, Mena was gone. There was a note on the bench that said my dinner was in the fridge, and she'd be back at eight thirty in the morning.

Opening the fridge, my eyes landed on the plate holding a steak I knew would be juicy and potatoes just the way I liked them cooked.

"Fuck," I grumbled to the room.

I knew I'd been a dick to her, but she should have called me.

Jesus, I remembered she'd caught the bus, and it was pitch-fucking-black outside. She knew I wanted to drive her to the bus stop, but instead of putting up with my arsehollery ways, she'd left to walk alone at night.

Slamming the door closed on the fridge, I went to go

to the front door to see if I could still spot her down the drive, but instead, the phone rang.

"Yo."

"How was your first day of work, son?"

"Next time you want to give the go-ahead to some bird I don't know to feed my son something he could choke on, don't. Or better yet, ring me, and then I'll tell you no fuckin' way."

"You finished?" Mum asked acidly.

Fuck me.

"For now."

"Right, my turn and listen good, child of mine. Your son needs his solid food now. He's at the age jar food won't do shit for him. You keep coddling him like you have been, it'll all turn to crap. He is a strong, good little boy, and Mena giving him food today should fucking show you that he *can* handle it, but it's your mind that's holding him back. It's your worry that will deter his growth," she snapped, but she hadn't finished. "I just bet you took all this shit out on a woman who doesn't need it. Mena is a good woman. She has experience with children and *you* picked her. The time I spent with her, I saw how much she would be great for Koda, how she would care for him like her life depended on it. Do not fuck this up, Kalen. You keep treating her like shit, she won't keep staying around for it. You're probably too full in your own head to notice the sadness lurking in her eyes. She's been through a lot, Kalen, and the last thing she needs is you being a prick about shit that *should* be happening anyway."

"I ain't here to *coddle* her, Mum. I don't give a crap about her sadness or anything—"

"Do you care about your son?"

"You know I fucking do," I shot back.

"Then loosen the goddamn ropes and let your son grow. Let him shine under her watch. You're a fantastic father, Kalen. The best. But I fear the worry you have will be harmful to him."

Shit. She was right, and I bloody hated she was.

"Still, didn't give either of you the right to try something on my son without my knowledge."

She snorted. "Like you said, you wouldn't have given us the go-ahead anyway. At least now, your worry should have eased knowing your son knows how to handle his food. Shit, you're his father, and you were like a goddamn vacuum at that age."

"Fuck me. I should never have had you come over today."

Mum laughed. "Maybe you shouldn't have because now Mena has my back on all decisions with Koda. Other than trying to help your son, did she do anything else wrong today?"

No. The fucking house was cleaner than when Mum did it. The meal she made looked edible, nothing like

Mum would have made, and my son... hell, there was a new light shining in his eyes, and it made me wonder if it was because of that woman today.

"Kalen?"

"No."

"Exactly. She will be an asset in the house. Not a problem." She gasped. "You didn't fire her, did you?"

"No," I grumbled.

"At least a part of your brain isn't so stupid. Listen, I'm leaving at the end of the week now I know things are settled with you, and I want to come back to see Mena still in the house. Don't fuck this up for me, for you, and especially for your son."

"As long as she never thinks she can take the place of Koda's mum."

Mum sighed. "My baby boy, no one would take Simone's place. We will all make sure of it. Simone will always be remembered, and Koda will always know she was *his* mum. But a child is allowed to care for more than one female. Besides, I doubt Mena would ever try to be someone she's not."

"She said it, but—"

"You accused her of this already? Boy, where was your head at? Fuck me. She has a lot to deal with and now putting up with your arse. I'll be goddamn surprised she'll be there when I get back. Stop being a dick, Kalen."

"Love you, too, Mum."

"You know I love you, even if you drive me insane." A smile was in her voice. "Now go have a shower. I can smell you from here and then eat your dinner. Mena told me what she was going to make, and I just bet you're dying to dive in… get it, Dive." She laughed. "Talk to you tomorrow night when you've finished work."

"You coming here tomorrow?"

"I know Mena had everything under control, but I think I will pop in, see what else Mena and I can scare you with." She giggled.

"Mum," I growled, but she'd already hung up the phone.

Shaking my head, I placed my phone on the table and went for a shower. Mum was right about another thing; I was dying to dive into dinner.

The shower helped my tense muscles loosen. I stood there, eyes closed, head lagging low with my palm pressed against the tiles. Letting the hot water run over my back, an image of sweet blue eyes flashed in my mind.

"Fuck," I whispered harshly.

My dick stirred, growing half-mast. Another image of long legs, soft blonde hair ran through my mind causing my dick to harden even more.

"Shit no," I growled. I was not fuckin' thinking about another woman. I conjured a picture of Simone in my mind and took my dick in hand. Slowly, I stroked up and down it. I forgot the last time I'd come. Christ, it was so long ago. The craving to rut struck me. I'd left it too long and I wasn't going to last. At least I was still going to enjoy it.

"Fuck," I clipped out roughly as Mena's face, then her body flashed into my mind, wiping away my image of Simone and causing my balls to shrink up. My stomach tensed as the feel of my cum drew down and squirted out the tip while I kept running my hand up and down my cock, faster and faster. Groaning, I pulled the last drops of cum from my dick and placed my other hand on the tiles, breathing heavy.

Now, I was pissed right the fuck off.

My mind shouldn't have gone there. Shouldn't have pictured *her*. In fact, it made me mad as hell.

"Fuck." I sighed into the shower, my jaw clenching, my hands balling into fists as I brought them to my sides and stood tall. "Fucking hell," I snapped before turning off the shower.

What in the Christ did I get myself in to?

CHAPTER SEVEN

ONE WEEK LATER

MENA

The first week went flying by. I had been scared to go back the day after Kalen yelled at me about Koda and his solid food. However, when I'd turned up, he seemed over it. In fact, as he was leaving, he told me I could give whatever I wanted to Koda, but I had to watch him like a hawk. He'd walked out the door before he saw my beaming smile. I found out later Judy had given her son a good talking to. Though, she added she wasn't sure he wouldn't still be a dick to me. His cold attitude didn't bother me. What kept me coming back was Koda.

I felt guilty for getting paid to be the housekeeper when really there wasn't much to clean up. The only rule I had was to stay out of Kalen's room. Still, there were only the dishes and laundry each day. Other than that, the house stayed pretty clean. Regardless, I also decided to vacuum, sweep, and mop every day while Koda had an afternoon nap. I swore Koda could sleep through a bomb going off. I didn't want Koda, when he started moving around more, to be doing it on a dirty floor.

On Wednesday, I asked if I could do some gardening and clean out the shed I saw in the backyard. Kalen said I could knock myself out with the garden, but there wasn't anything to tidy in the shed.

By Thursday, my luck had run out. I'd managed to dodge Kalen when he got home and got out of the house before he mentioned him driving me to the bus stop. However, Thursday night he'd just taken Koda to his bedroom to get ready for bed, and I'd managed to make it to the front door before he came out and barked, "You move out that door, there will be trouble. It started spitting on the way home. I'll drive you to the bus stop, or better yet, I'll drive you home. Just give me time to get Koda changed and I'll get him in the car."

"No, you really—"

"Not another word, Mena." He glared.

Glowering back, I shot back, "Fine."

Thankfully, after he dropped me off, he didn't stick around waiting for the bus to show because he wanted to get Koda home. The walk took me an extra twenty minutes to get back to my car. He did it again Friday, and it had been pouring rain. By the time I'd made it to my car, I was drenched, shivering, and cold to the bone.

To warm me up, I did something I hadn't done in a very long time. Laying back flat on the back seat, I placed one foot to the floor and the other I lifted up to the top of the seat. My heel rested against the back platform. I felt ridiculous. I'd never had the urge to touch myself in the car before, but I couldn't stop. My hand went to the front of my pyjama pants. Slowly, I slid my hand inside, only to gasp from the cool touch of my hand. Still, I kept gliding it down. I was already wet, and I knew it had something to do with a certain male I worked for. While I arched, gasped and moaned, running my finger up and down, in and out and around my clit, two steel eyes consumed my mind. Eyes that were hard, heated, hot, and wanting *me*. The orgasm I had was like nothing I'd felt before and thankfully, it left me exhausted.

When I woke the next day, I was surprised I didn't wake up with a cold. To prevent one, I made sure I stayed inside the car all weekend, and ate all the fruit and vegetables I had left. I had no intention of going out into the terrible weather.

In my solitude, those steel eyes kept making appearances in my foolish mind.

On Monday, I chose to drive to Kalen's; I didn't want a repeat of Friday since it was still raining, and I also had some washing to do. My clothes from Friday were still damp and smelled out the car. After parking out the back, away from Kalen's vehicle so he wouldn't think to look in mine, I made my way in through the back door.

Kalen was in the kitchen finishing up Koda's breakfast of Weetabix crushed in milk. Kalen seemed to be handling the change in Koda's food well. I just had to make sure it stayed that way.

"Morning," I offered at the doorway, heat lighting my cheeks at the memory of touching myself while my boss's eyes had flashed in my mind.

Kalen grunted and then looked over. "You look like shit. Did you get any sleep last night?"

Sighing, my head dipped forward, eyes to the floor in shock at how rude he was. Did he seriously say that? How he ever starred in my twiddling fantasies was a surprise. I had to get my head checked.

Actually, I hadn't got much sleep. The wind had been fierce the night before, and every noise made me jump out of my skin.

"Charming as ever I see," I mumbled, ignoring his comment. "Did Judy get away okay?"

"Yeah, fine." He went to spoon another bite to Koda,

but he turned his head away and started grumbling. "He's been doing that since yesterday."

Walking straight to Koda, I felt his forehead. "He seems a little hot. He could be coming down with something."

"Shit."

Without thought, my hand went to Kalen's shoulder when I said, "He'll be okay. We'll take good care of him." When Kalen glared down at my hand, I quickly removed it and stepped back.

Over the last week, I'd noticed how consumed Kalen was with Koda. He worried over every little thing. It made me wonder if it was because something had happened to Kalen's wife. Still, I realised I overstepped my bounds touching him.

He was a good-looking man. A woman would be crazy not to see it. But his coldness when his wall erupted around him was enough for me to know to steer clear of him, or I'd have my head bitten off. I wasn't there to help him; my responsibility was Koda.

Going to the fridge, I grabbed out Koda's water bottle before saying, "If anything changes in Koda, I'll call you." Knowing I wouldn't get a response, I busied myself in the kitchen while he said goodbye to his son. Once he'd left, I went to Koda to pick him up out of his high chair.

Quieter than usual, Koda leaned his head against my chest. He was definitely coming down with something.

By the end of the day, Koda ended up with a blocked nose, watery, red eyes, and he'd become more irritable. He hated it every time I wiped his nose and even more when he couldn't breathe from it when it came to bottle and naptime. He didn't get much sleep at all. His appetite was small; all he wanted were soft things, which I realised when he pushed away his favourite cracker. No doubt he had a sore throat.

Poor boy.

Come five, I rang Kalen because after using his computer, I worked out what Koda would need for his cold.

"Yo."

"Kalen, it's me, Mena." His annoyed sigh was loud, so I went on before he could say anything. "Koda has come down with a cold. Can you pick some things up for him?"

"Fuck. Yeah, what?"

"Vapour rub for babies, a humidifier, the chemist should have them, and we'll also need a nasal aspirator."

"Got it. Be back soon," he said before he hung up.

Placing the phone down, I went back to Koda, picked him up from the floor, and sat him on my knee. He cuddled right in. "Daddy will be home soon, sweet boy, and he'll bring things that will help." It sucked an eight-month-old couldn't have medicine to help with all the other pains, but if things didn't improve in the next day or so, I would ask Kalen to take him to the doctors.

I heard the car pull in before moments later, the front door opened. "You didn't lock it again," he said with a growl before walking to us and leaning in to kiss Koda on his cheek. "Hey, buddy," he whispered in a soft tone that made my heart warm.

Clearing my throat, I informed him, "Actually, Koda and I got up just before to unlock it for you since it's still pouring out there." His reply was a chin lift as he stepped back. I saw the worry in his eyes for his son. Standing, I said, "We'll take the stuff you got in his bedroom. He hasn't slept much today because his nose it all blocked. I think you may have a rough night ahead. How about I run him a nice warm bath with some lavender lotion mixed in it. It'll help soothe him while you set up the humidifier?"

"Sure."

Koda seemed to enjoy his bath at least. After it, I wrapped a towel around him and went back into Koda's room where I found a freshly showered Kalen. The humidifier was already going. Placing Koda on his change table, I quickly dressed him in his nightwear, leaving the front open.

"Can you pass me the vapour rub?" I asked, holding out my hand. It was slapped on it. Opening the lid, I had Kalen hold the tub while I scooped some out with my fingers. I gently rubbed it onto Koda's chest, then shifted him to his side for a little on his back, all while Kalen watched on quietly.

"Um, this is the hard part." I cringed.

"What do you mean?" Kalen barked.

"Can you mind him while I wash my hands?" He nodded. When I got back, Kalen was leaning over his son talking softly to him. "Okay," I started and then opened the box for the nasal pacifier. "You, um, either do this or hold his head."

"What the hell are we doing with that thing?"

It was obvious he hadn't seen a nasal aspirator before. Pointing to the small end, I explained, "This bit will go into Koda's nose, and then we squeeze this end, and it will suck his snot out."

It was comical how Kalen paled straight away. "You're fuckin' with me, right?"

Shaking my head, I bit my bottom lip to stop my laughter and then mumbled, "No."

"That is wrong on so many levels. I will not do that or let you do it to my kid," he bit out and moved in front of Koda like I was a threat.

Rolling my eyes, I asked, "Do you want Koda to be able to breathe?"

"Of course," he clipped out roughly.

"Then you have to do this. He doesn't understand how to blow his nose to clear it, Kalen. He needs our help."

"Fuck." His eyes went to the ceiling, and then he

glared back down at the pacifier. "Jesus motherfucking Christ."

"Kalen?"

"Okay. All fuckin' right. But I can't… I won't do that." He pointed to the aspirator like it was a gay magazine.

"I'll do it, but you'll need to hold his head still for me," I said. He nodded and moved to the side of the table. Koda, possibly sensing something was about to happen, started crying. "It's okay, sweet boy. We'll help you." Smiling what I hoped was a reassuring smile, I leaned over Koda while Kalen gently took his son's head in his hands. Placing the end in his nose, I quickly sucked the snot into the pacifier.

Kalen dry retched and then heaved again.

Koda stopped crying and seemed surprised by the sound.

When I moved to his other nostril, Koda started struggling. Looking to Kalen, I saw his head was faced away, and he seemed a little green. "Hold him still, please."

"Just do it already," he growled, but his hands controlled Koda's movements enough for me to do it again. Koda cried on this one.

Kalen's hands disappeared, and more dry heaving sounded behind me.

"You okay?" I asked with obvious humour in my voice while I picked up Koda to console him. Turning, my eyes landed on a bent-over Kalen, his hands on his knees and he was breathing deeply through his nose.

A giggle bubbled up and came out. I couldn't stop. Seeing tough Kalen react like that over some snot was the funniest thing I'd ever seen. Soon Koda was laughing with me. Not that he knew it was at his dad's expense.

"Woman," Kalen barked. I quieted, and then he must have remembered and heaved again, which caused me to giggle once more. Kalen stood tall and turned to me. "That was the sickest thing I've ever seen, and I've seen some shit in my life." My hand went over my mouth to try to stop laughing. Kalen's mouth quirked at the ends. "Stop laughing at me." I couldn't. The visual kept popping into my mind. He groaned, shook his head, and… was that a chuckle? It was. He threw his head back and laughed. In fact, I stopped laughing just so I could watch him. It was a beautiful sight.

"Jesus, you are never to mention this shit to anyone. I nearly lost my stomach for fuck's sake." He shook his head and held out his hands to Koda, who looked exhausted. Koda went straight into his dad's arms and grabbed his beard. "Please tell me I won't have to do that through the night?"

I shrugged. "Not sure. It seemed to help him right now. I'm sure he's ready for bed as soon as he's had his bottle."

"You're right." He nodded, looking down at Koda, who

was resting his head against Kalen's chest. A chest that was firm. A chest I hadn't taken notice of until then. And a chest that I shouldn't be looking or caring about. "Let's hope to Christ we don't have to repeat that. I don't think I could do it on my own." He looked up to me. Thankfully, my eyes were already on his face. "You got a phone yet? In case I need you to… ah, come back and do that sick shit again?"

Smiling, I rolled my eyes and said, "I would come back and help, but no, I don't have a phone yet." I would as soon as payday came which was Friday.

"You need to get onto that. No woman should be without a phone."

"I will." I nodded. Our eyes stayed connected. I needed to look away, needed to appear unaffected. I didn't like the spell I was suddenly under when his steel eyes were soft and warm. When his face was relaxed and not scowling at me. But I didn't, so, of course, I saw the wince, and his face harden to the Kalen I knew.

I should have looked away first.

Then I wouldn't have felt the hurt when his upper lip raised in disgust.

Starting for the door, I said, "I better go. See you tomorrow and good luck tonight."

"Do you need a lift?" His voice was cold once again, and his tone told me he thought I was nothing but a burden.

"No. I drove. My car is out back." Wanting to get away, I didn't even say goodbye to Koda. Instead, I walked from the room and then out of the house into the pouring rain. Luckily, I'd got some washing and drying done that day. I had fresh clothes in the car to change into when I was parked back in my spot.

That night was another restless night of sleep. I was concerned for Koda, and I hoped Kalen was handling it all okay. What was also on my mind was Kalen and his quick change of attitude. It was as if he forgot he didn't like me for a moment. I knew the following day that he'd be back to his usual cold self. Why would he hide that part of himself from me? Whatever the reason, it was a loss that rested deep inside of my hollowed stomach. The part where he was carefree, with no deep dark thoughts consuming his mind.

Still, I knew there was nothing I could do about it.

I WAS RIGHT. Kalen was back to being himself the next day. By that night, Koda wasn't so ill, and it took only four more days for the sweet boy to be back to his cheeky self. If anything, the cold seemed to have awoken something inside of Koda because it was just a week later, I walked in to a crawling Koda.

A gasp escaped me. I got to my knees and cried a

happy cry, clapping my hands in front of me. "You clever, boy. Look at you go." He crawled right up to me where I picked him up and hugged him close. "You're amazing, little man." Smiling, I looked up to Kalen who, I wasn't surprised, scowled down at me. He quickly disappeared out the front door after that. I was used to the scowl—not that it got any easier to see. Every time my eyes caught it, I'd release a troubled sigh because I didn't understand his hostility towards me. Well, I sort of did. It seemed Kalen hated seeing the affection I'd show his son, but I wouldn't stop just because of a mean look. I was proud of the little boy I'd gotten to know and care for, so of course I would show Koda just how amazing I thought he was.

We soon discovered Koda liked to get into everything he could. That was until Kalen came home with *more* childproof locks, which he put on just about everything.

CHAPTER EIGHT

FOUR MONTHS LATER

DIVE

I was going to just have a small party for Koda's first birthday, but Mena, with Mum's help, talked me into a big shindig. Well, not too big. I didn't want too many at the house, which could cause Baxter, the dick, wanting to harm Hawks, to take notice on why so many Hawks brothers were travelling our way. If he was still keeping an eye on us in some way, the travel to mine wouldn't fly under the radar. There was no way we wouldn't notice we were being watched, but fuck if we knew what was going through that fucker's head.

At least the day was going to be a good one. The sun was out, which caused me to get the BBQ out of the shed. I bought a heap of meat to grill while Mum and Mena said they'd take care of the rest of the food.

Only, that was after Mena came to me and asked if I minded if she came to Koda's party. At first, I did. But then she'd been pretty cool with him, and she was going to be in his life for a while, so I told her I didn't care either way. My answer was a dick move because what I should have said was that she was more than welcome to come. She did so much for Koda, and I knew she deserved to spend his special day with him as well.

I couldn't seem to turn off my prick when it came to her.

After Mum had come back from her trip, she'd been for dinner once at the weekend and asked Mena to be there as well. After Mena had left that night, Mum had the gall to state I was a bastard to her because I was attracted to her. I'd snarled at her, telling her she didn't know what she was talking about and ordered her out of the house. She left with a huff, telling me to get my head out of my arse. It pissed me off even more knowing she was right… about it all.

The front door opened, and Mena walked in after ducking out to get changed. A yellow summer dress hugged her figure causing my dick to jerk. She saw me, smiled, and started for the kitchen. I glared, shook my head, turned, and went out to the backyard leaving her to do whatever and Mum in Koda's room getting him changed before everyone showed.

Stupid, fucking cock. Do not take notice of that shit. Never, you hear me.

My head came up from talking to my dick when I heard vehicles approaching. I'd asked them to come in cars and not their rides, so they didn't attract more attention. Call me paranoid, but I was.

Just as I got around the front, I saw the first car pull up, and then another four parked around it. The one I actually smiled about was Talon and his fucking minivan. I understood it; he had Wildcat, Cody, Maya, and the twins, but shit, it was hilarious to see the president to all Hawks driving a goddamn minivan.

When he jumped out, he glared and snarled, "Not a motherfucking word." I threw my head back and roared in laughter, then laughed even harder after Drake jumped out of the back and yelled, "Not another mothertruckin' word."

Wildcat's door flew open. She got out and walked around to face her husband. "Did you hear that, honey?"

"Kitten." Talon smiled down at her.

"No." Her hands went to her hips.

"Mum," Maya started. "Drake didn't actually swear,

and he knows not to because Dad would kick his ars—" Cody placed his hand quickly over his sister's mouth.

Zara spun to her kids and glared. She threw her hands up in the air and yelled, "I give up." She spotted me and started coming at me. I was in her arms next. They tightened around my waist, nearly knocking the breath out of me.

"Boss, your woman's mauling me again," I yelled.

A gasp sounded from the front porch. Looking up, I saw Mena standing there. With wide eyes, she looked out to all approaching men. Never thought to mention I was part of an MC. But she'd know it now when all my brothers were wearing their cuts.

Wildcat stepped back. I watched her look from Mena to me and then back again. "Don't fuckin' think it," I warned.

Wildcat faked surprise. "Who me? I don't know what you're talking about."

Before I could say more, Hell Mouth shouted, "Where's the booze? I'm gettin' tanked. It's date night, ladies. No kids for us tonight and all the fun we can have." She threw her arms in the air and hooted. Her man Griz tagged her by the neck with a hand and pulled her close, then whispered something in her ear. She nodded and smiled up at him. "Okay, not too tanked. We both still gotta perform tonight."

"Aunt Dee." Cody groaned, shaking his head and looking to the grass.

"Oh, shush, kid. You're old enough to know about sex—"

"Low, what's sex?" Rommy yelled out.

"Oops," Hell Mouth said, and then after the quick hug she gave me, she bolted inside, where I noticed Mena had also disappeared. Hell Mouth probably knew Low, Dodge's woman, was going to kill her.

"Low?" Rommy asked again.

"We'll talk about it later, sweetheart. Why don't you kids go find Koda? I'm sure he's looking forward to some lovin' from you all." Rommy skipped off gladly, grabbing Maya's hand along the way while Tex and Cody grabbed the twins on the way past. All greeted me with a "Hey," before they walked around to the backyard.

"Sugar, all I suggested was for you to take your weight off your feet," Blue said suddenly.

"Are you saying I'm getting fat, Blue? Because I swear if your kid makes me fat, I'll sit on your face just to suffocate you." She glared at her man before stalking my way where she kissed me on the cheek and said, "Good to see you, Dive."

"Ah, yeah. Congrats I hear are in order?"

"Thanks." She smiled and made her way inside with Zara and Low.

My brothers surrounded me. Fuck, it was good to see

them. Even though Talon, Griz, and Blue were from the Ballarat charter, and I saw them even less, it meant a fucking lot that they'd come all the way here for Koda. And shit, I didn't realise I'd missed my brethren from the Caroline Springs charter as much as I had; Dodge, Vicious, and even Lan was there.

"Good of you all to make it," I said, my voice thick with gratitude.

"Any fuckin' time and for any fuckin' reason," Talon said with a serious look on his face. I gave him a chin lift and greeted all the fuckers with a pat on the back.

"When you heading home?" Blue asked.

After a shrug, I said, "Not sure. Things are good here right now." Some would call me a big lickable pussy for not fighting my memories at home. But I couldn't. I wasn't ready. Everything reminded me of Simone and how I lost her. Too much pain came with it.

"The reason the leggy blonde in the house?" Vicious asked. Dodge shoved him hard. He teetered sideways but caught himself. "Fuck, sorry."

"Not a problem, brother. But no, nothing to do with it at all." Glancing to Talon, I asked, "Where's Stoke and Killer and their crew?"

"Couldn't make it. They said they'd get up here soon, though."

Everyone turned when another car came down the drive and stopped. Already I could see Pick and Billy in the front. The back door opened, and Josie got out, then Nary.

"Headin' in. Got some beer, brother?" Vicious asked.

Stupid kid and his stupid ways for staying away from the one thing he wanted. And now the loss, having her move on, would fuck him up even more. We all knew Nary was the one person who would have done anything for him, yet he'd screwed it all up. No one understood his reasons, but one fucking day, I'd have a talk with him and tell him life wasn't worth wasting.

"Yeah, in the Esky out back."

He was out of there even before the others had made it to us, as were my other brothers, leaving me with the new arrivals. When they got close, Nary gave me a hug with a hello and then went on inside. Josie came forward with a sad smile and then took the last step to wind her arms around my waist.

Pick and Billy stayed behind their woman. With my teeth clenched hard, I looked down at Josie while she looked up. "How you doin', babe?" I asked and even that hurt. I hadn't seen her since the funeral. The woman before me knew what loss was. She understood how my insides were still raw and bleeding.

"I'm getting there." She nodded. Tears pooled in her eyes. "She would have been so proud of you."

"Don't," I bit out.

"Right now, Simone would be looking down upon

this and seeing how you've become an amazing father."

"Josie," I groaned. My head went back, eyes to the sky as they filled with tears.

She sniffed. "She'll always be in our hearts, Dive. I'm sorry I haven't got up here to help with Koda. I want to get to know him and be close to him because he has a part of my best friend in him." Looking down, I saw she felt guilty when her eyes wouldn't meet mine.

"Nothing to apologise for, babe. We both went through a lot, but you more, being so close to losing Rich." She bit her bottom lip and nodded.

"No loss is compared. We both feel it, but… we both need to remember life does go on. It may take a month, a year, even two or five, but life does go on, and we learn to cherish what we have and live like each day is the last. With no regrets."

"I'm trying, Josie. I'm trying."

"So am I." She stepped back and wiped her face. "So am I," she said again before Billy came forward to claim her with his arms around her waist. Shaking her head, she added, "I guess I should apologise for being so deep and ruining everything before it got started."

"No, woman." I smiled. "Nothing is ruined. Come on, let's go see Koda."

"I'd love that."

THE DAY PROGRESSED WELL. My brothers and I spent most of our time out the back with the kids. Koda was having fun with Maya, Rommy, and Ruby while the boys played football around them. My son was at the stage where he was pulling himself up on everything. After he'd started crawling, it seemed like he just kept wanting to do more and more.

The women gossiped inside while getting shit ready and no doubt drilling Mena on everything about me. I bet I'd get a talk later when they find out I'd been nothing but an arse to her. Lunch was awesome. Mena sat at the other table, the guys and I pulled out of the shed, with the women, Mum, and kids. She even fed Koda. It wasn't even her working day, and she still took care of him.

She threw her head back and laughed at something Hell Mouth said. The sight was fucking amazing. Never had I seen her laugh that hard or free. Hell, not even when she was giggling at me when I was dry retching after that snot issue Koda had.

Her shoulder length blonde hair and bronzed skin went well with the yellow sundress. Goddamn, I'd been a huge dick to her, and she still kept coming back. I knew why. She was in it for Koda, and I appreciated that she was. Fucking lucky she was the one I employed. Mum loved her, and it looked like my brothers' women did also.

Wasn't hard. She never said a bad word about anyone.

Shit, she didn't even swear. I'd love to see her riled up, see what she said or how she acted. Her face flushed with frustration and anger. I knew being a bastard to her was wrong on so many levels. She didn't deserve it, but it was a front for how confused I was. I was attracted to her. My cock knew it every morning she arrived. It was like he wanted to wave good morning. But then… then I'd remember my heart was supposed to belong to Simone, and being attracted to Mena made me fucking crazy mad, so I took it out on her.

Jesus Christ.

Guilt sat low in my belly. I shouldn't even be looking at Mena the way I was. Simone had been dead only a year, and already my eyes were straying. I was a cunt.

Dragging my eyes from the table and back to my brothers talking around me, I shook my unwanted thoughts away. It sucked not all of our large family could make it, but things were busy. Julian and Mathew were occupied with minding Griz's kids, and they even took them away for the weekend. Simone's parents said they'd be up later in the week, but had prior arrangements so had to miss Koda's party. I think it also had to do with the fact they knew my biker brethren would be there. They didn't feel comfortable around them.

No matter. For once, I was finding myself smiling and feeling somewhat happy.

For then anyway.

MENA

When Judy sent me out the front to see if Kalen needed any help, I didn't expect to see women with huge men wearing biker vests.

Biker vests.

Kalen's friends were part of a real bikers' club.

Before I could embarrass myself by saying or doing something stupid in front of them, I quickly ran inside and closed the door, leaning against it.

Judy saw me from the kitchen, where she stood with Koda in her arms. She laughed so hard, I thought she was going to pull something. Once she got herself under control, she ignored my glare and said, "I guess, my boy forgot to tell you he's a part of Hawks MC?"

"Why yes, Judy, he did. In fact, you didn't say anything either."

She shrugged. "I didn't want to scare you off when you'd just started, and honestly, I ended up forgetting you didn't know."

No wonder he'd asked those questions at the start. Oh, my God. Were those the women who had others after them?

"Stop worrying. You'll find out they're a wonderful bunch. Come and help me here." She gestured to the table where the fruit sat ready to be cut up for fruit salad. My heart felt like it was in my throat. I'd been worried for some time about meeting Kalen's friends. Even if I was only the hired help, they'd still judge me. Then, seeing they were bikers, more nerves fluttered through my stomach. What happened if they hated me? I was sure Kalen would appreciate their input about the woman taking care of his son.

Sugar, what would happen if I lost my job because they thought I was terrible?

"Mena," Judy whispered, just as I jumped from the front door opening, nearly cutting off a finger. Glancing to Judy, she added, "Breathe and calm down. They'll love you like I do." My eyes brimmed with tears. It had been so long since someone said they loved me, and coming from Judy, a woman I looked up to, meant so much. She smiled sadly and patted my cheek, which Koda thought was funny, so he did it too. At least that put a smile on my face.

"Hey, ladies, what's shaking?" A tall woman, who was stunning, with long light-blonde hair and blue eyes strutted in. She gave Judy a hug before standing next to the bench eyeing me.

"Mena, meet Deanna, or as the boys like to call her Hell Mouth," Judy introduced.

"Hi," I said hesitantly with a small smile, only it vanished when her eyes narrowed on me.

"Who are you, and what do you have to do with Dive?"

Oh, I got it. Dive must have been his biker name. Still, if it was, why Dive? It didn't make sense.

"I'm, um, I look after Koda when Kalen is at work. I also do the housework."

"You fuck Dive over, us women will come down on your arse. He's been through enough. He doesn't need—"

"Deanna, that's enough," Judy snapped. "You do not come in here and threaten Mena. She does an amazing job, and I won't have you scaring her off."

I stuck my chin out and glared at Deanna myself. "And I would never do anything to hurt Koda or Kalen."

"Yep, she'll do." The change threw me off. I dipped my brows when she smiled. "Give me some cutie pie. I need some Koda lovin'." She reached out for Koda, but he cringed back into his nanna's arms.

"He's still funny with people he doesn't see much," I explained.

"I'll bring him outside in a second. Meet you out there, Deanna," Judy said. Deanna rolled her eyes and did as Judy said. Before Judy left, she turned to me and said, "She's all talk, that girl. I met her once a long time ago, and her bark is bigger than her bite. Don't let her talk shit to you. Stand up for yourself with these women. Get me?" she asked.

"Yes. Thank you, Judy."

"Anytime, love." She smiled and then headed out with Koda while I finished the fruit salad. We'd already made pasta, Greek and potato salad. Then with the fruit, for after lunch, we'd made a mud cake, an orange and poppy seed cake, and a cheesecake. For the kids, there were some brownies and cookies.

I had hoped the rest of the people out the front would have walked around to the backyard, but I knew I had no such luck when the front door opened to three women, all gorgeous in their own way and all different.

"Hi." The one with long wavy dark hair smiled. "I'm Zara and married to Talon. This is Low, who will be getting hitched to Dodge, Dive's best friend," she explained, pointing to the black woman. "And that's Clary. She's with Blue and is expecting." Clary waved.

"Hi, it's great to meet you all," I said and then slid the cantaloupe into the large serving bowl with the rest of the fruit. After wiping my hands, I added, "I'm Philomena, but everyone calls me Mena."

"I hear you're Koda's nanny and their housekeeper. How are you finding working with Dive?" Clary asked.

Biting my bottom lip, I gulped and then said, "It's good. Koda is the best baby. Did you hear he's crawling now? Has been for a little bit. He's into a lot more than usual. I'm sure you can all imagine. I saw all the children outside."

"Okay. We'll get to the part about you not mentioning Dive in any of that. But right now, I own two of the mob of kids, Rommy and Tex. Well, they're Dodge's niece and nephew, but we have custody over them when their bitch of a mum kicked the bucket. The rest belong to Zara. There's Maya, Cody, then the twins, Drake and Ruby. She's just recently popped out another, but that's her brother's baby," Low said before she popped a piece of watermelon in her mouth.

What parallel universe just walked in the front door?

Zara had a baby to her brother?

Clary and Zara started laughing, and Low asked, "What?"

Shaking her amused head, Zara explained, "She wasn't really my brother's baby, but my brother's husband's baby. My brother is gay. Of course, they can't have kids, so I offered to have one for them. Which is also why they aren't here today. Plus, they're minding Deanna's two children."

I gushed, "That is so nice of you. What's her name?"

"Aeila." Zara smiled.

"That's really beautiful."

"They picked well." Clary nodded.

"Anyway," Low started. "Back to Dive. You told us how things are with Koda. What about Dive?"

"Um…" Thankfully, the front door opened, or not so thankful when four good-looking, but large, scary men walked in.

"Yo," the one who came up and stood behind Zara said to me.

"Hi," I squeaked.

"Where's my woman at?" the older one asked.

The women shrugged, so I stepped up and said, "Ah, if you mean Deanna, she went outside after she threatened me."

The man actually chuckled. "She can't help herself." He shook his head and headed outside. My eyes followed him. When I turned back, all the other men's eyes were trained on me.

Can somebody say EEEK?

"Mena." Zara caught my attention. "Behind me is Talon. That's Dodge and Blue. The one who left was Griz. I promise they look rougher than what they are."

"Okay," I drew out. The men chuckled.

The front door opened again, and a younger woman walked in with a smile on her scarred face. Even with the scar going from the corner of her mouth up to her cheekbone, she was stunning.

"Men out. We have things to talk about," Low announced. The men grumbled about bossy women getting their arses tanned. Still, they listened and headed out back, which actually made me smile. Big tough bikers doing what their women wanted. It was very sweet, not that I would ever mention it to the men's faces.

"Mena, Nary. Nary, Mena. Dive's housekeeper and Koda's nanny," Low rushed out. "Right, down to business. How's it been with Dive, not Koda. Just Dive?"

I shrugged and looked to the bench.

"Tell us if we're being too bossy," Clary offered.

"Why in the fuck are all the women in here, and I wasn't invited?" Deanna yelled.

"Shush you. We've already heard about you threatening Mena—"

Interrupting, I said, "No, it wasn't a threat as such—"

"Yeah, it was." Deanna grinned. "But you passed, plus she has a green flag from Judy. I was out back, and all she could talk about was Mena this, Mena that. I had to come in here just to get away."

Low clapped her hands to get everyone's attention.

"Can we all just stop talking, besides Mena telling us about Dive?"

"Good call." Deanna nodded. "Spill, woman."

Sighing, I said, "There's nothing to say. I'm his employee. He pays me to take care of the house and his son. I cook, I clean, and—"

"Stop!" Deanna barked.

"You mean to say he ain't made a move on you?"

"Dee, it's only been a year since Simone passed." Zara glared.

Deanna rolled her eyes.

"Oh, God. Koda's mum died?"

Nary's hand came over mine. "You didn't know?"

Shaking my head, I whispered, "No. We don't talk, honestly."

The front door opened once again, and Kalen came in with another woman and two other bikers; they both looked like they would kill anyone if they breathed the wrong way.

The woman came up to Nary and placed her hand around her waist. Nary's arm went around her shoulders.

Dive stepped up and barked, "Things ready for lunch?"

"Yes." I nodded. He grunted and kept walking out the back with the other two bikers.

"Oh, shit." Low whistled in the silent room after all the men had once again left.

"Is he always like that?" the new woman with red hair asked. "Sorry, I'm Josie and the two men you saw are Calen and Eli, also known as Pick and Billy."

"Mena, and yes, he's always like that."

The room fell silent again. All women in their own thoughts.

"Josie also forgot to mention the men she said are hers, as in she's bonking the both of them," Deanna blurted.

My eyes widened, and everyone started laughing.

It was just what we needed, and somehow, I knew Deanna knew that, because when I looked at her, she winked.

THE DAY WAS AMAZING. I loved all of Kalen's friends. They couldn't get over the fact I called him Kalen. But I said I found it strange to call him Dive since I didn't know he was a biker. Then I asked why his biker name was Dive. All women laughed around me, even Judy. Then Zara said, "You don't want to know, or better yet, you should ask him."

They were so different in personality, yet, they all complemented each other. When one got too much, either Deanna or Low, the others brought them back down. They were wonderful. I was glad Kalen had people like them around him, but I didn't understand why he moved away from it. I knew Zara, Clary, and Deanna were in Ballarat, but the others were close to Kalen, and I could tell they thought highly of him. Some of the stories I heard… didn't describe the man I knew. They described someone with a lot of laughter in his life, a man who loved trouble, but in a good way.

Losing Simone, who was also Josie's best friend, really did something to him.

That kind of pain I could understand. Had felt even, and still felt some days.

It just seemed to fester inside of Kalen.

Later, after I put Koda down for his nap, which was the only nap he now had during the day, I was walking down the hall towards the kitchen when I paused, hearing male voices.

"Mena's pretty hot." I recognised Dodge's voice. I rolled my eyes.

A snort answered. "If you like the type who annoys the hell out of you, with a voice that irritates me every time she talks. Who's always lookin' scraggly and is putting on weight like a fuckin' freight train? Sure."

Arching my shoulders in defeat, my head dropped forward. With watery eyes to the floor, my hands wrapped around my stomach. Each word was like a knife to the gut, a new stab wound each time he put me down. My heart, not wanting to be left out, felt as though a hot poker was being slashed at my skin across my chest.

I knew he didn't like me. I just didn't know how much.

My hand went to the wall to steady me. My legs seemed to shake like my insides were and suddenly, I felt cold all over.

He really hated me.

Why did he keep me around?

Why would he say such things?

How could one person be so mean?

"Bit harsh there, brother. It seems to me you're just—"

Dodge didn't get to finish because foolishly, I had stumbled forward. The movement and shuffle brought their attention to me.

My heart beat loudly in my chest. My ears rang. My hands shook. But I stood tall as both men came into the living room just off the hall.

"Fuck," Dodge muttered roughly.

Licking my dry lips, I cleared my throat and stammered, "S-sorry to interrupt. I-I just wanted to say Koda is sleeping and… I must go."

"Jesus, Mena," Kalen groaned.

"Do you mind I say a quick goodbye to your friends?" *Before the devastation can take over.*

"We're doing cake when he wakes. You have to stay for that," he demanded.

Thing was, I didn't have to do anything he said.

"No. I have other… I have to be somewhere." My chin lifted. He seemed to know when I did that, I wouldn't back down, and there was no way I would.

Not after *those* words.

"Mena—"

"It's okay. You can say goodbye to them for me." As fast as I could, I walked around them and went to the front door.

"Mena, fuck, wait."

With my hand on the door handle, I looked over my shoulder and informed him in an aloof voice, "I'll be back Monday for work, Mr Brooks."

He flinched.

Good.

It didn't match what I was feeling inside, but it was something at least.

He didn't come after me. I was stupid and stomped on the small amount of hope I had that he would rush out the door for me to stop. So when he didn't and I was halfway walking to my car in the bushland, I cried. Tear after tear fell, and they wouldn't stop.

I'd heard harsh words before. Growing up poor, it was the normal to hear them.

They'd just never stung as much as Mr Brooks's did.

Never would he be Kalen again.

He was my employer and nothing else.

Since Mark's death, I never thought warmth would have touched me again, but it had; Koda and even Kalen were the reason for that. Until that night, it was the coldest, most lonesome night I had felt in so long, and a part of me even felt it was worse than what I had felt before.

CHAPTER TEN

DIVE

My arse got chewed out by just about everyone that afternoon. They didn't make me feel worse, though. I was already feeling like the biggest fucking prick. Her face… her sweet face was… crap! Fuck, it hurt to see the pain I'd put there.

I should have chased her. Dodge urged me to, but I couldn't. I didn't know what to say to her. How could I come back from being such a lowlife? It had been all lies. Everything I said was a bunch of bullshit, and Dodge was just about to call me on it when we'd heard the crash in the hallway, and then she was standing there. She'd heard every fucked-up word.

My heart and body begged me to reach out to her, but my mind refused.

Christ.

She'd called me Mr Brooks before she'd left.

Mr fucking Brooks.

I'd lost her.

Before I even had a chance to have her.

Have a chance to redeem myself for the cockhead I'd been, because I was just worse than a cockhead, and any redemption seemed completely out of my grasp.

When everyone started to leave, Dodge hung back until the last couple, and I knew I was going to get another earful. The worst that day was from my mum when she told me how disappointed she was with me. Apparently, Zara had been inside at the time, hidden around the corner. She told the women, and then *boom* everyone had something to say.

Low was sitting in the car with Tex and Rommy, while Dodge and I stood on the front porch, and Koda was crawling around the front grass enjoying himself.

"What you gonna do?" he asked finally. I shrugged. "Your mum was right. It's time to stop being a dick to her."

Clenching my teeth, I clipped out, "I can't."

He scrubbed a hand over his face. "You fuckin' can, but you're being a stubborn prick. Just because you find the woman attractive doesn't mean anything bad against Simone. Hell, it's been a year."

My hard gaze zeroed in on him. "A year. One goddamn year, and yet it seems like it was just yesterday."

He stood tall, crossed his arms over his chest. "It seems like yesterday because you won't get past anything else."

"Just leave it, brother."

"I worry about you."

Sighing, I said, "Don't."

"I can't not." He shoved me. "You're my brother from another mother, dude." We both chuckled. And then he added, "Stop being a dick to her and apologise. That's all any of us want. We ain't trying to set you up with her. Fuck, you're the one who brought her into your life. You don't have to let her in, but treat her like a normal human being. Not like someone who's shit on you."

"I will." I had to. The hurt in her eyes flashed in my mind over and over, and seeing it wouldn't rest from my mind.

WHEN SHE SHOWED MONDAY, she looked like a zombie. A cute one. But still a zombie. She had bags under her eyes, and her skin was paler than before.

Hell, maybe the distance was for the best.

I was still too fucked-up on Simone to start shit with a woman I didn't know. Even if she was one hell of a woman, who took care of my son with her whole heart.

Then again, when she walked in and offered me a nod with no eye contact, no greeting, fuck, not even a, "Mr Brooks," I knew the distance wasn't for the best. The interaction we'd had before, even when it was small, was a highlight of my day.

Why was my guilt about betraying Simone the one thing I couldn't let go of?

Because Simone was a good woman.

I paused at the thought. Was she? When she didn't tell me about our kid, when she took away my chance to be with her through everything. When *she* chose how *she* wanted everything. Even if she thought she was doing best for me, it was a selfish action. Because it meant she didn't have to see how crushed I was, she didn't have to be there for *me*.

Thinking about Simone that morning had me walking out the door without saying anything to Mena. I should have apologised. I should have told her the truth.

But I didn't.

I walked out thinking about myself once again.

Thinking of *my* feelings, *my* emotions, and *my* memories.

All day, it played on me.

All day, I was caught up in my head, which annoyed

the fuck out of me because it made me feel disgusted in myself. I wasn't the only one with feelings, and I was sick to the stomach about what I said to Mena and how I acted towards her from day one.

She didn't deserve any of it.

When I got home, Koda was in the living room on the floor playing and watching TV. I heard Mena in the kitchen. With a quick hello to my son, I headed for the kitchen and stood in the doorway.

Her head was in the fridge, her arse up in the air.

My cock hardened.

Jesus. He certainly wasn't confused like my mind was.

When she stood and turned, she met my eyes for a second and then moved to the bench and said, while drying some dishes, "Your dinner's in the fridge. Koda's is also ready. I was about to give it to him. I didn't realise you would finish early."

My boss had sent me home an hour earlier because I'd been useless all goddamn day.

"Um, I've done your washing. If you would like to strip your bed tomorrow morning, I'll wash them, and if this weather stays, they should dry quickly." Because I'd asked her to stay out of my room, which was the one rule I'd given. I didn't want to scare her with all the cameras and shit I had going on in there. She took a breath and went on, "You being home, does this mean I can leave early? I'd like to go and do some things in town."

"I'll give you a lift. I noticed you didn't drive again," I offered in a softer voice. Her cheeks lit with fire. I wanted to know why, but then her chin tipped up and out, and she glared. I knew the colour on her cheeks was from frustration or anger, probably a bit of both.

She opened her mouth to say something, but Koda made his presence known by crawling around my legs and into the kitchen. Silently, we both watched him grab a chair and pull himself up. He decided to slap his hands on the seat. I smiled down at my boy. He wanted attention or food, and the way he ate these days, my guess was food.

Mena also knew this. "He wants his dinner probably, so I'll leave you to it and make my way home." She moved off, even though I hadn't said she could have the extra hour off. Couldn't blame her really. She was used to taking off as soon as I got home.

Because I was a cunt.

It was time I stopped.

"Mena—"

"Mr Brooks, please don't. It's better this way anyway—"

"No, it's fuckin' not. I hate hearing Mr Brooks come from your mouth, Mena, so you need to stop that shit and stop with the cold shoulder. I know what I said was heartless, but I want you to know none of it was true." She snorted and her jaw clenched. I went on, "Hell, Mena, you need to believe I was speaking outta my arse. Dodge was talkin' about you, and I said some shit to get him off my back. Even he knew I was full of it." Nothing, she said nothing, and I'd even lost her eyes at the end. "I want things to go back to the way they were." Even though she wasn't looking at me, I saw her eyes roll. "What, Mena? Tell me what you're fuckin' thinkin'. Tell me I was a rat bastard. Tell me how I can fuckin' fix this."

Her head spun to me, her glare heated. "You can't," she snapped. She threw her hands up in the air and said, "Maybe with time I'll forget about it. Just... let me be, please."

"Will things go back to what they were?"

She shook her head, but said, "Sure." Biting her bottom lip, she mumbled to herself, "It's not like you were nice before."

I took it. I deserved it because I hadn't been anything but a prick.

"Let me give you a lift."

"No, thank you."

She let out a small sigh in relief when Koda started crying for his food. She said, "You'd better feed him."

I didn't stop her when she gave Koda a kiss on the cheek and me a defiant look, before she headed to the front door and then out it. I wanted to go after her, but I knew I'd get nowhere. So I'd just have to prove I was going to change. I was going to prove I wasn't a total dick, and one day, I'd admit what I really meant with those words she'd heard me say to Dodge that day.

That I thought she was stunning.

After I'd fed my boy and got him to bed, the phone rang.

"Mum," I answered.

"I was around your place today. I tried to tell Mena you're not usually a wanker, but she didn't want to hear it. But, Kalen, her eyes told me your words had cut her deep. Tell me you fixed her today. Tell me."

Sighing, I told her, "I apologised."

"Thank fuck you saw some sense. Now you give her time. Show her my child is the sweet, good boy I brought up."

"I've already decided to calm things between us, Mum. I don't need another lecture about my attitude towards her."

"Okay, Kalen. I'll shut it. Now when are Simone's parents coming up?"

"Sunday."

"I'll come over and cook—"

"Mum."

"Fine. I'll ask Mena if she can come early and help me out by cooking something decent."

"Not sure if she will." Though if Mum asked, I could see Mena helping her out.

Mum laughed. "Oh, she will. I tried to make lunch

today while she was busy doing some washing. She witnessed I wasn't good at it, yet she still tried it. Lost count of the times she cringed and pretended she loved what I made. Heart of gold, that girl. That reminds me, did you know she does her washing at your place also."

"No." I was never home when she did household shit. "Why?"

"She said her washing machine wasn't working. I told her you wouldn't care she was, but she asked not to say anything to you about it."

"Fuck, I don't give a shit. I bet she doesn't have a phone for herself yet either. What in the hell does she do with the money she gets off me?"

"Can't say I know."

"Maybe it's time I find some more shit out about her."

"Go in easy, Kalen. We can't lose her."

Mum had always wanted more kids and a daughter to call her own, but after I was born, she'd discovered she couldn't have any more. It'd been hard enough to fall pregnant with me. I wasn't blind to see she saw Mena more than just my worker. She cared for her deeply.

Wasn't hard to do.

CHAPTER ELEVEN

TWO WEEKS LATER

MENA

My back was killing me. I'd slept the wrong way. Being cramped up in the back seat obviously didn't help. Actually, I was surprised it hadn't happened earlier. I hoped with some movement, my joints would click into place, so I risked walking and having Mr Brooks offer to drive me home. I also chose to walk because I thought Koda might like to take his first bus trip into town. Besides, I knew how to dodge around his offering to drive me home. I had managed it for the last few weeks. Then, if all else failed, I'd just make a run for it.

It was Saturday, a day I didn't work, but I'd mentioned to Mr Brooks about how I thought it would be good for Koda to start some swimming lessons while the weather was good. He agreed as long as I was the one to teach him.

Since Koda's birthday and those things he'd said, Mr Brooks had changed. He wasn't super great, but I knew he was trying. He didn't bark at me so much. When I'd cooked for his family and Koda's grandparents, he asked me to stay for the lunch. I didn't.

I wasn't a part of their family.

The reason I helped that morning was so Judy didn't kill anyone. It was no wonder Mr Brooks agreed to have me cook for Koda and himself. Judy was terrible in the kitchen. I was sure she knew it, which was probably why she ate out a lot with her friends, but I didn't say anything to her the day I forced down what she'd cooked for lunch.

Thankfully, she hadn't tried again.

I knew Mr Brooks was sorry for what he said, and I knew I shouldn't hold a grudge over it, but the words still lingered in the back of my mind. I admitted to myself they hurt more because I liked him in a way my heart fluttered wildly in my chest. Unfortunately, those stupid feelings didn't go away after he'd crushed me. I wished they had. I wished I hated him, but I couldn't. Not when I witnessed what he could be like when he was himself with Koda.

It seemed I was an idiot when it came to a certain man.

Still, as long as those words kept shooting around in my mind and heart, I could keep my distance. I could pretend nothing he did fazed me.

I was there for Koda, which had become my mantra.

As I made my way down the driveway, I saw Mr Brooks already outside with Koda. My feet halted. What was going on? They were never outside to greet me. Picking up my pace, I called out, "Is everything okay?"

"Yep, you ready to go?" he asked, looking down at me through aviator sunglasses, which I hated to add, he rocked with his jeans and a black tee.

"I'm sorry?" I asked, stopping in front of them beside his car. I looked in it. The door was already open, and a bag was sitting on the seat.

"Swimming."

"Yes, I thought I was going to be taking him. In fact, I was going to take Koda on his first bus trip, which is why I walked." I reached out, to take Koda's hand and kiss it. He giggled. Then I noticed Koda was already in his full-body swimsuit.

Pushing his sunglasses to his head, he leaned in and ordered, "Nope. Hop in."

"But—"

"Dada," Koda yelled. My eyes widened, and I gasped.

Clapping, I grinned like a fool and said, "Yes, baby boy, that's your daddy. Can you say Mena? Mmmena."

A deep chuckle hit me. "He's been doing that all morning. It's like all of a sudden he woke up and decided he was gonna talk."

Taking Koda's cheeks in hand, I lay kiss after kiss over his face, "You're such a good boy. You're so smart, Koda. Smarter than any kid your age."

"Mena, get in the car, please."

Maybe it was the please or maybe it was the warm eyes I looked up into, but I found myself moving the bag and sliding into the front passenger seat.

Once he had Koda strapped in, Mr Brooks came around and jumped in, started the car and began down the drive.

"Are you swimming?"

"Nope, just coming to see how he goes."

That was actually sweet.

"Dada, Dada, Dada," Koda sang in the back.

I leaned around and smiled brightly at him. "I'm going to buy you something special in town for being so awesome, Koda Brooks."

Suddenly, my eyes teared. Koda was growing up so fast. It was amazing to watch. If I was that excited over his first word, I couldn't imagine what I'd be like when he started walking.

When we pulled up out front of the local outdoor swimming pool, I got out and went around to help Koda, but his dad was already there, so I reached in for the bag and threw it over my shoulder.

"Oh, no," I exclaimed after walking through the gate.

"What?" he asked.

"I forgot my towel." Where was my head at? How stupid was I?

"I have a spare."

"Mr Brooks—"

A deep rumble, sounding something like a growl, hit the space between us. "For fuck's sake, call me Kalen." His head went back; his face tipped to the sunny sky and he cursed again. When he looked back to me, he reached out and took hold of my wrist. Could he feel my pulse take off from his touch? *Old men in spandex, old men in spandex.* My heart slowed with the picture in my mind. He then added, "Mena, I would feel better since I use your first name if you would use mine."

Dazed, I nodded.

"Thank you." He smiled.

Fight it, Mena. Fight that damn smile like you have been since he started torturing you with it for the last two weeks.

I nodded again.

As soon as he stepped back, the spell broke. I shook my head and pulled off my sundress. I was already wearing my black one-piece bathers. With my eyes on Koda, I clapped, and he reached out to me. Kalen gave him right over, and I headed for the solar heated swimming pool.

Slowly, we walked into the water. At first, it took my breath away. Not wanting to scare Koda, I didn't let it show. He watched with wondrous eyes when we went deeper and deeper into the water. He smiled, laughed, and wiggled in my arms. A couple of times he tried to jump away from me, reaching with both hands out to splash the water. I knew then that Koda was going to love to learn to swim.

DIVE

My eyes stayed glued to them. I was glad Mena didn't look at me when she claimed Koda from my arms because she would have seen the heat in my eyes. Then again, they'd been hidden behind my sunnies, which I was fucking grateful for because I got to watch them both, not just Koda enjoy himself, but also Mena. I got to watch when she slipped out of her sundress to show her hot body with curves in the right places. When she'd first shown on my doorstep, she was skin and bone. Now she had curves I wanted to get to know.

And fuck no, I was not pushing that thought away because of guilt.

Simone always knew I was a huge fan of a woman's body. Besides, they were only lustful thoughts. I wasn't in the right place to act on them.

Still, the show was amazing to watch.

Even better, when an hour later, they got out of the water and I followed every drip running down her sexy legs.

"He did such a great job, Daddy. You should be proud." Mena smiled before sitting Koda down on my lap.

Shit. Focus.

Wrapping his towel around him, I said, "Yeah, he looked like he was enjoying it." I picked him up, turning him to face me.

"Dada." He smiled before latching his hand onto my beard to give it a tug.

"You're a real little swimmer, buddy." Pulling him closer, I blew raspberries onto his neck, making him squeal. Glancing up to Mena, I was disappointed to see she had the spare towel wrapped around her body. "You ready for some lunch?"

"If you want to get going, I can take the bus back home."

"You're not hungry?"

"No, I'll get something later."

"Woman." I sighed. "Let me get you some lunch as a thank you for his first swimming lesson."

"I don't want to get in the car all wet. I was going to lie out in the sun for a bit anyway, get dry, and soak up the rays before it changes." She looked to the sky. Dark clouds were coming in even though the temperature was still warm.

"Don't worry about the car, Mena."

"Kalen, I—"

"Fine. We'll grab something here at the kiosk. Then I'll take you home."

"Um, okay, thank you. But I need to grab something from your place, so I'll get a lift back there and then catch the bus."

Standing, I handed over Koda. "I get the feeling you don't want me near your place, Mena."

Pink touched her cheeks. "No, it's not that. I… um… It's just…"

"How about I go get the food while you think of something."

"Fine," she snapped and actually stuck her tongue out at me. It took everything in me to walk off and not bite down on that tongue.

There was something going on with Mena, and I was going to get to the bottom of it. I trusted her with Koda.

But I needed to know what she was hiding. It was a guess, but I reckoned it had something to do with where she lived. So while I ordered the food, I activated a plan.

We all ate lunch sitting in the sun. Not much conversation flowed, but it was nice just sitting there with her. Later, she disappeared to the toilet, only to come back with a toy truck.

"Where'd you get that?"

"I ran across the road to the shops. I promised Koda I would get him something." She sat down next to him. As soon as he saw the truck, he started waving his hands around and squealed.

Fucking lucky she'd put her dress on before slipping out and heading around other people. She was already getting ogled by enough men around the pool. I was half tempted to join her. With me by her side, the other dicks would know not to approach her. Fuck, they'd probably approach her anyway. I clenched my hands into fists in annoyance. *Calm the fuck down, it hasn't happened yet... Not unless it has and she just hasn't said anything to me.*

Running a hand through my hair in frustration, I grumbled under my breath with a few choice swear words.

The car ride was quick and when we pulled down the drive, and she saw Mum's car sitting there, she relaxed. No doubt she thought she was going to be in the clear and slip away. I'd let her, but little did she know I was going to follow her. I'd called Mum earlier and told her what the go was. She was all for it.

We pulled to a stop and got out. Koda was in my arms when Mum came out on the front porch.

"Afternoon. How'd he go?"

"He was amazing," Mena cried excitedly.

"Is that why he's got a new truck?" She smirked.

"Mena got it for him for saying his first word."

"What? He talked? What did he say?"

"Dada." I grinned proudly. I'd been working with him every night, and finally, he'd shocked the shit out of me and came out with it that morning.

Koda mimicked me and cried, "Dada." Then he smiled.

"Oh, what a sweet voice for such a little charmer," Mum cooed, grabbing Koda from my arms. "We need to celebrate. Dinner out somewhere, with drinks. No, let's go take a trip, let's—"

"Mum, maybe another day. He's had a big swim. He's probably ready for his nap." She eyed me and then Mena, who stood beside me looking at Koda with a smile on her face.

"Right, of course he is." She nodded. "I'll get him to bed. It was nice seeing you today, Mena." Mum turned and fled into the house.

It was almost comical how Mena paled. She looked from Mum to me, back to Mum closing the front door to me again.

"Um, the bus will be coming soon. I better get going." She spun and started off.

"I thought you had to get something from the house."

She waved over her shoulder, and called, "It's okay; I'll get it Monday."

My bet was there was nothing in the fucking house. She was trying to dodge a lift off me again. I stood there, watching her walk down the drive. I didn't go after her, not yet. I waited until she cleared the corner, and then I took off running into the bush, hoping to catch her before she got to the bus stop. Then again, I highly doubted she even got on the bus, which meant she lived near my house somewhere. The problem with that was there was nothing out there but shrubbery.

Instead of being in my own head, I should have looked into Mena more. Though, what she brought to the house—a smiling, carefree, stunning woman—was what kept me from looking deeper. I couldn't bullshit myself that it was also because I wanted to keep my distance from her. I'd known her for a little over four months now and what I knew wasn't enough.

Slowing my pace, so she wouldn't hear me coming, I was about to duck out on the road that led to the bus stop until my ears picked up footsteps to the right. The sound led away from the bus.

Turning, I followed the footfalls. Then she made it

easier by humming. What she was humming, I didn't have a clue. Still, it sounded sweet.

My eyes caught sight of her, and if she turned around, she would have spotted me in the distance, but she didn't. She was in her own little world. Goddamn it, I'd have to make sure she took more notice of everything around her. You never knew when something could fucking happen, and I didn't want Mena taken by surprise.

Except by me.

Where in the fuck is she going?

Nothing was in the direction she was heading.

She disappeared behind a tree. I kept walking, and then I heard a fuckin' car door open and close. Worried I'd lose her, I started running and soon came into a clearing where a beat-up Torana sat.

My eyes scanned the area; there was no sign of Mena.

Stalking to the car, I threw open the back door. My eyes narrowed on all the shit in it as Mena began to scream.

"What the fuck?" I growled.

"Kalen." She clutched her heart before tears pooled in her eyes. Her cheeks heated, and then she covered her face with both hands, crying.

CHAPTER TWELVE

MENA

He'd found me. He'd followed me and now he knew what a disaster I was. After he scared the bejesus out of me, I broke down. I was ashamed he'd seen me at my worst. Ashamed he was looking in at everything I owned.

"Out," he barked.

Great. He was back to barking at me.

He probably saw me as nothing but trash.

Was he about to turn me out like trash as well?

"Mena." He growled the word. "Get the fuck outta the car, now."

His snarling tone got me to wipe my face and scoot

my butt from the back seat to stand just before him.

And I meant *just* before him.

Kalen hadn't stepped back. He was still leaning with one hand on the roof and the other on the opened back door. When I stood, our chests nearly touched.

My bottom lip wouldn't quit trembling. However, I jerked my chin out and up, and even though my eyes teared again, I glared up at Kalen Brooks.

"I'm a good person. I've never done anything to harm Koda in any way—"

"Jesus Christ," he clipped through clenched teeth. Then he took a deep breath and asked, "What are you talking about, woman?"

"Even though I'm… I-I'm living in my car, it doesn't mean you can fire me." I sniffed in a shuddering breath.

"Keys," he snarled.

"Kalen," I cried. "I promise I'll go and get away from you all. I won't do anything, but don't turn me in for being on this property."

"Keys," he demanded.

Sighing, my head dropped forward. "I'm sorry, please."

"Mena. Fuckin' keys now."

Nodding, I knew I was in deep shit. He'd had enough. All I could do was go along silently. He was probably disgusted a hobo had been taking care of his son. Wanted to take me to the police station and get me away from Koda. My heart plummeted at the thought.

Grabbing the keys, I passed them over. I was surprised when he placed a hand on my waist and moved us back so he could slam the door shut. He grumbled some things under his breath as he moved us to the door of the front passenger seat.

When he opened it, he barked, "Get in."

My eyes went to the seat, to him, to the seat, and back to him. "Why?" I questioned, my bottom lip quivering again.

I watched a muscle in his jaw tick. He was seriously pissed.

Throwing my hands up in the air, I snapped, "Fine." And as I ranted, he came around to the driver side, got in, and started the car. "What are you going to do, Kalen? The police can't do much about me being on public property, except maybe give me a fine I can't— Kalen, I'm sorry I applied for the job and didn't tell you where I was staying. I'm sorry if you think I've done anything wrong by Koda. I would never want to do anything..." I trailed off when I noticed he'd had the car heading down his driveway.

He parked and got out. I stayed where I was, or at least that was my intention if he hadn't come around my side and yanked my door open. He leaned in and took my arm in his hand, tugging me out of the car.

The front door opened, and Judy stepped out. "Koda's asleep." She stopped and took in her son's expression.

"What's going on?" Her hands went to her hips, and then she looked at me, saw I'd been crying, and said again, "What's going on?"

We made it up to the front porch before Kalen said between gritted teeth, "She's been sleeping in her goddamn motherfuckin' car this whole bloody time."

Judy gasped. Her hand went over her heart. "Oh, love," she whispered to me, her eyes filling with tears.

"It's okay, really, Judy. It's fine."

"Shut it," Kalen ground the words out.

Pulling my arm from his, I stepped away from him and glared. "Don't tell me what to do. I've had it up to here." I gestured with my hand to the top of my head. "I know you're pissed about having a homeless person minding your son, but I—"

"Mena," Judy called. I looked at her and she shook her head.

"I'm making a call. You deal with her," Kalen ordered his mum and walked into the house.

"He's not mad at you, love." Judy tried to reassure.

"It sure seems it."

She stepped up and wound her arm around my shoulders. At first, I stiffened, but then hugged her middle. "When he sees something he doesn't like, he gets pissed. He didn't like seeing you living in your car. He's not pissed at you, but at your situation, and if I know my boy, he's in there doing something to fix it."

"He can't fix it, and I wouldn't want him to." I sniffed back my tears. Only they got the best of me because someone was caring enough to hug me. I ended up crying into Judy's shoulder. "He doesn't even like me."

Judy chuckled and said, "You'll have to take that up with him, love."

The front door opened with force making us both jump. Kalen stepped out and said, "You're on the couch tonight. Tomorrow, I have some brothers coming up to help me shift some shit around in the shed. It used to be an art studio of some sort. You'll live in there until you're back on your feet. If you think you're not gonna listen to me, start thinking again. I have your keys to your shitheap of a car. You can't go anywhere."

My body froze.

My mouth wouldn't work for words; it just kept opening and closing.

I was glad he turned on his heels and went back inside, closing the door behind him, because then my body unstuck, and when it did, it hurt.

A sob ripped from my throat, my eyes closed, my hands went to my belly, and I bent over as tears fell freely.

I wasn't alone.

Someone cared.

I wasn't alone.

He was doing something to help me.

He didn't hate me.

I wasn't alone.

"Oh, God, oh God." A body folded around me, arms around my back and waist. I was feeling too much all at the same time. My head didn't know where it was at, as well as my heart.

"Oh, lovely Mena. My dear girl. You're okay. You're going to be okay," Judy whispered into my ear, only I couldn't answer her.

Life had thrown me a hard one, so I couldn't agree I was going to be okay.

Still, right then, I did feel it. I grabbed hold of that hope, the strength Kalen offered, and I held on. I cherished it while I could.

Judy's weight left my back, and next I was being lifted into strong arms. I knew it was Kalen. Hiding my face into his neck, I curled my hand around the other side of his neck. I wanted to say thank you. I wanted to tell him how much it meant he cared enough. But I didn't. The emotions were still working their way through me, causing me to cry nonstop. He carried me in and planted my butt on the couch. As he was still crouched over me, he slowly dragged his hands from my body. His warmth left me until I felt *his* hand on *my* neck, where he gave me a gentle squeeze. I offered a nod, hoping he would take that as my reassurance I'd try to get myself under control.

Seeming to understand, he stepped back and

mumbled low to his mum, "I'm gonna get shit ready for dinner."

"Okay, my boy," Judy whispered. She sat next to me, slipping some tissues into my hand.

When Koda woke later, it was a sound that woke the house. Judy and I had been sitting on the couch quietly. I'd eventually stopped crying and was cleaning my face. Kalen had been in his own silence in the kitchen. I wasn't sure what he was doing, but from the sound of it, it was nothing. No pan or dishes clattered as if he had been getting things ready for dinner.

Judy was the first to move to get Koda from his room. When she came back out with him, she placed him in my lap. It was just what I needed—to see Koda groggy and grumpy. I loved it when he woke like that because each time, he curled into me for a hug until he was awake enough to run amuck.

That time, I wasn't sure if he sensed I needed a longer hug. But he stayed on my lap for a while. Eventually, he pulled back and patted my face before giving me an open mouth, sloppy kiss on the chin. Once he did, he wiggled free to the floor and crawled off, looking for his dad. I knew when he found him because he cried out, "Dad." Looking to Judy, we both shared a smile.

The afternoon was spent in our own heads while we watched and played with Koda. Kalen kept his distance and did his own thing until he took Koda with him down the street to get some takeaway for dinner. Judy let me have my mind. She didn't ask questions; instead if we did talk, it was about Koda and her next trip, which was coming up soon.

It wasn't until later when Koda was tucked into bed, and Judy had left, that the fluttering in my stomach started. It was because Kalen and I were alone. I'd never really been alone with Kalen.

Hearing his footsteps coming my way, my heart skipped a beat. He came out carrying a pillow and blanket, placing them on the end of the couch. My eyes stayed on the bedding. I wasn't ready to look up into his eyes.

"Want a beer? I'm havin' one," he asked, which shocked me. I thought he would head back to his room to leave me alone. Then again, he saw what a wreck I'd been and probably thought I wasn't stable alone, or there was still a chance once he got a beer, he could retreat to his room.

My eyes flicked to his, and I nodded before turning to face the TV. It was on, but the sound was down. It had been all afternoon. No one interested in turning it up.

An opened beer bottle was shoved at me. I took it and then watched with wide eyes as Kalen moved the bedding into the middle of the couch so he could sit at the other end.

After he had taken a drink, he stated, "We gotta talk, Mena."

I gulped back my own drink and nodded.

"How'd it all happen."

With my eyes glued to picking at the label on the bottle, I told him everything. "My parents died when I was young. I was an only child, and so were they. I had no one except my best friend, Mark. I moved in with him. He had no one after his only family passed as well. It was like we were meant to be in each other's lives. We, um, later, down the track, he asked me to marry him. I didn't want to lose the only person I had left, so I said yes. I did love him. I just wasn't in love with him." God, why did I tell him that? "We never had much, and I never wanted anything except for us to be happy. However, Mark wanted it all. Over the years, he'd accumulated a lot of debt. I wasn't strong enough to say no. I didn't want him upset with me. Foolishly, I let him sink lower and lower into debt. I thought with both of us working we would eventually pay it off." Biting my bottom lip, I added, "Then Mark died, and I was left with all the debt." I shrugged. "I live in my car so I can pay it off."

Kalen moved. He leaned forward, resting his elbows on his knees, his beer in his clasped hands in front of him. "Why not still live in a place and pay off the debt slower?"

"I have a mark against my name. No one will rent to me. Besides, I'm okay with my situation. As soon as I'm in the clear, I'll start building a new life. At least, I have to believe that."

"You live in a fuckin' car, Mena," he sneered, his upper lip raised.

"I know, Kalen," I snapped.

"For how long?"

"Nine months or so."

"Fuck me. How in the hell have you kept safe doing it?"

"By learning, moving around."

"Anyone fucked with you?"

"No."

"Don't lie to me, Mena."

Sighing, I admitted, "One time, but nothing really happened. He scared me. I got in the driver seat and was out of there before he got in the car."

"Shit situation, babe."

Babe.

He'd said babe.

What? Why? How?

"I know," I whispered.

"Should'a been smarter."

"I know." I nodded.

"Gotta stand up for yourself."

Rolling my eyes, I snapped, "I know!"

"Like I said, you're in the shed by tomorrow night. Do not fuckin' think of paying me shit. You cook every day.

That's your payment. Koda would be lost without you around. I won't let my kid feel that. You're staying. Even if you tried to leave, I'd drag you back."

"I wouldn't, Kalen. This… you, I-I'm so grateful for what you're doing." Sitting up straighter, I looked at him and said, "I can't say thank you enough, but you'll see. I'll cook the best meals you know." I smiled. "So much so you might want to look at starting the gym."

A smirk touched his lips, and then he rolled his eyes. "Get some rest, woman. Brothers will be here bright and early."

Feeling silly because I was happy to be anywhere but cramped in the car, I saluted him and said, "Righto, captain."

"Nutball," he muttered before standing and walking down the hall to his room. Then he called out, "Your car's out back unlocked. No one would bother taking that piece of crap, so you can get whatever you want outta it, but you ain't getting' the keys."

Too happy to feel offended, I simply grinned. Maybe, just maybe, Kalen didn't hate me after all.

After I went out to the car to grab my sleepwear, I came back in to make my bed. I knew that night I would be going to sleep smiling, feeling safe, warm and over-the-moon happy.

CHAPTER THIRTEEN

DIVE

She was dead to the world sleeping on the couch. It gave me a chance to watch her without her noticing. She blew my mind. How could someone who was sleeping in their goddamn car have a heart of gold? If it was me, I would have been bitter and miserable, but not Mena. She still turned up at the house with a positive attitude and a smile on her gorgeous face.

Fuck me. She'd tucked her shoulder-length hair behind her ear to get it off her face. I wanted nothing more than to lean over her, run my hands through her hair, and then take hold while she sucked me off. Which was the image I wanked to last night.

Did I feel guilty taking my cock in hand with thoughts of Mena?

Hell no.

How could I when she was everything pure and sweet.

She was in a shit situation and having her move into the shed would hopefully help her out more. At least she'd have a bloody roof over her head. Not a goddamn car roof either. Bile had risen in my throat when I'd realised where she'd been sleeping, and I knew I'd do anything for her never to sleep inside a car again.

The house had a spare room, but I knew if she was constantly in the house, I wouldn't be able to hold myself back. Neither of us were ready for where I wanted things to go.

But it'd happen.

One day soon.

If I didn't chicken out and let guilt take hold.

My head lifted from Mena on the couch to the door, where I heard Harleys coming down the drive. I shifted off to the kitchen before Mena woke and saw me staring at her like an obsessed tool. Besides, I had to get Koda's breaky ready; he'd be awake soon. My kid was the best fucking sleeper. I couldn't have been luckier with my son. I'd heard so many bad stories about people getting no sleep with their kid waking through the night. Not Koda, he liked his sleep like his dad.

My whole body locked when I heard movement

behind me, and I found myself picturing Mena coming up and placing her hands on my waist while she got to her pretty toes to kiss my neck.

Fucking hell.

"Morning," she said groggily.

Turning, I had to smile at her messed-up hair and half-mast eyes. She wore a pair of track pants, low riding on her hips and a tee that was two sizes too big for her. Still, she looked good enough to eat.

Shit a brick. I had to stop my thoughts.

"Morning. Sleep okay?"

She smiled so wide I got all teeth. "The best sleep I've had in a long time."

Chuckling, I said, "Just wait until you're in a bed tonight."

Her head jerked back. She wiped at her eyes and said, "But I don't have one."

"Don't worry about a thing. You wanna go check Koda? My brothers—" There was a knock on the front door.

"I'll get it," she just about sang. A good night's sleep did wonders for her. I hadn't seen her that bubbly before. Then again, I never gave her the opportunity to be like that.

God, I'd been a cunt.

I heard the door open, and then she said with an audible sexy-as-fuck gasp, "Oh, my God."

Not liking her breathy tone at fucking all, I stalked into the living room to see her standing in the doorway looking up at Dallas.

"You gonna cry?" Dallas barked.

"Um, no," Mena offered. I came up behind her and smiled at my scary-as-fuck brother.

"Good, I hate cryin' women." He lifted his head and sent me a chin lift. Dallas wasn't one to smile. "Brother, good to see you."

"You too, man," I said and looked down to Mena, who was still staring up at Dallas. "You wanna let my brothers through, sunshine?"

Her whole body jerked. She shook her head and then looked up at me before she nodded and took a step back. Dallas walked in. Quick to follow were Knife, Muff, and Beast.

"There's more of them," I heard Mena mutter.

After a quick greeting to all brothers and sending them into the kitchen for coffee, I walked to stand in front of Mena, who seemed to be holding up the opened front door. "You good?" I asked, my lips twitching.

"Ah, yeah."

"They aren't gonna hurt you," I said quietly.

Her hand came to her chest. "Oh, I'm not worried about them. I've just never seen so many good-looking men in one room." Colour touched her cheeks, her hand moved up to cover her mouth. She was embarrassed she'd blurted out what was meant to be a thought, no doubt.

Annoyance burned low in my gut. She thought my brothers were good-looking, the bastards. She'd better well count me in there also, or shit would hit the fan.

"Maybe you should take Koda to Mum's today," I ground out low.

She bit her bottom lip and looked up at me with uncertainty in her eyes. "Do you want me out of the way?"

Fuck.

"No, shit, I—" Thank fuck that was when Koda started calling. "Look, go grab him, get changed, and see how things go, okay?"

"Okay." She nodded and ran down the hall.

Running a hand over my face, I walked back into the kitchen. "The ride up good?" I asked as Muff slid a mug of coffee my way.

Dallas grunted. "If you mean were we followed, fuck no. We know the drill, man. But you gotta think one day soon brother about coming back. Isolated up here, even with all your camera and security shit, is a risk. Being within your brothers' reach is better than anything. Even you should know this."

Dallas didn't talk much, and when he did, people listened. Beast didn't talk at all. Though he got across what he wanted to say with texts or gestures.

I knew Dallas was right, but I'd been thinking it for a while, getting back to Caroline Springs. Still, something in me wasn't ready.

"I know, brother. I feel it, and soon I'll listen to it, just not yet." His reply was a chin lift. "Everyone know what the plan is?"

"Yeah, not sure we understand why you want your shed set up as a room, but we're more than willin' to help a brother out. The delivery of furniture should be here by lunch time," Muff explained.

"Who's the woman?" Knife asked, a smirk playing on his lips. The dick.

My hand tightened around my mug, and I raised it and took a sip. "Koda's nanny and my housekeeper."

"Damn fine." Knife grinned. It was my turn to grunt before I turned away and added, "Let's get this shit done." Then they'd fucking leave and forget all about Mena being damn fine. Bloody woman being too fucking sexy for her own good that even Knife saw it through her over-sized sleepwear and her hair all over the place. If she wasn't going to head to Mum's with Koda, then I'd have to keep her busy with other shit.

Mid-morning, the side door opened, and Mena walked out with a tray of coffees. Fuck me up the arse. She was wearing denim shorts and a tight tee. I didn't know she fucking owned clothes that actually fit her body.

"Coffee break?" she called.

Knife bloody rushed over to her side. "Let me help you with that, baby." He took the tray from her hands while I watched her cheeks heat.

Stalking over, I barked, "Where's Koda?"

She gave me an annoyed look and said, "In the living room. I put down a plastic table cloth, and he's playing with Play-Doh."

Shit, I was doing it again, but fucking Knife was pissing me off with how he was panting after her.

"Maybe change your clothes," I suggested quietly. Knife coughed back a laugh. I glared at him, and Mena gasped.

"Why?" she whispered.

"You've never worn shit that hugged your body before. Why start today when my brothers are here?" I asked and wished to Christ, Knife would be struck down by lightning seeing the smug smirk on his face.

"It's the weekend, Kalen." Mena glared up at me. Her hands went to her hips, and I felt like getting in her face and placing my hands over hers.

"So?"

As her cheeks pinked, she got close and leaned up to whisper, "I only have a few clothes. These are my weekend clothes. This and the sundress that I wore yesterday."

I was a cunt once again.

"Right," I said. I closed my eyes but felt her move back. My eyes opened to see her looking at me. "Thanks for the cuppas, sunshine." I smiled.

Her tinted pink face was back, and I goddamn liked that I caused it. I wondered if she'd blush seeing me naked. It had me thinking about how I could make that scene happen, so I could find out for myself.

"Um, I'll bring out some lunch later."

I gave her a chin lift. She took a glance to Knife, who was smirking away, and turned, walking back inside.

"Why she need a room?" Knife asked.

"She's had a hard time of it lately," I said with a shrug.

"Why didn't you tell me she was yours?"

We started back to the other brothers before I answered, "She's not."

"Sure, brother. Think I might test that theory out later."

Stopping still, I looked at him. His laugh was loud. The fucker was riling me up and nothing else. He wouldn't do shit. Actually, he was full of shit. Just liked giving me hell for not admitting to myself what Mena was.

Hell, what was she?

Nothing yet. Like I said, it was too soon. I had to see how things went with her being around all the time. She could have a habit I hated. Then again, she could end up hating me.

Handing out the coffees and even the bloody cookies she'd put on the tray for everyone, my mind went to one thought.

A thought that made me smile.

A thought that caused my heart to stumble over a beat in eagerness.

And that thought was making Mena mine.

Though, I had to calm everything down and go slowly. I didn't want to screw anything up by starting something and then have stuff about Simone pop back up, possibly causing me taking it out on Mena.

She didn't deserve it.

She was too sweet and she deserved sweet back.

She was my sunshine in the darkness.

CHAPTER FOURTEEN

MENA

Something was different with Kalen. Ever since I woke up that morning, I noticed a new light to his eyes. What had caused the change I didn't know. And I didn't mind not knowing because I was enjoying it too much. All except when he barked at me when I'd gone outside with coffee. Then he'd calmed, and the light was back when I mentioned about my clothing situation.

Sunshine.

He'd done it twice now.

Sunshine.

And each time was something special. It got my heart racing, my clit tingling, and my cheeks heating. Even when he was cruel and mean, my body was addicted to everything Kalen related. He consumed my mind. Everything I did—washing, cleaning, tidying, and playing with Koda—Kalen was there in the back of my mind. That smile. His eyes. His voice.

Oh, God. How was I going to survive living so close to him?

An engine caught my attention. Picking up Koda, we went to the window to see a big truck pull up out the front. Kalen walked around from the back and greeted the driver once he got out.

Pointing to the truck, I said to Koda, "Truck. *Broom, broom*. Truck." Then I pretended to place my hands on a steering wheel and drive along a bumpy road, jiggling Koda up and down in my arms. He loved it.

My breath caught in my throat when I saw what was being pulled from the back of the truck. It was a bed. Then a couch. Then some drawers. A TV and stand, and a coffee table.

I was out the front door and striding to Kalen. He was holding up his end of the coffee table when saw me coming, so he stopped.

I got close and whispered, "What are you doing?"

"What'd'ya mean, sunshine?"

The man at the other end, Beast I think, looked everywhere but at us, which I appreciated. "I-I can't afford these things, Kalen."

"Did I say you were paying for them?"

My head jerked back on my shoulders. He couldn't be that nice. He couldn't have done this because I was a good housekeeper and nanny… then again, I was a good cook, and the Brooks's boys loved to eat.

"Dada," Koda cried. My breath hitched when Kalen leaned into his son, who was in my arms and kissed him on the check. He didn't pull right back. Instead, he got in my face and said, "Not one word about this shit, Mena. Just get in there and make us some lunch." Then he moved back, adjusted the coffee table, and sent a chin lift to his biker brother. Apparently that meant get walking because he did.

Watching them move, I knew I shouldn't have when my eyes trailed over Kalen's body. He was fit, very fit and the sight of his back, his arms, and his butt walking while carrying something was a sight I could stare at all day.

Maybe, if he was still a dick to me, my mind and body wouldn't be obsessing over him in a way an employee shouldn't for her boss.

Rather than standing there like an idiot, I went back inside with a struggling Koda. He wanted to go be a man with his daddy. He saw other men around and thought that was where he should be. The poor monster didn't know he couldn't play with the big boys while they were doing the heavy lifting and moving around too much.

For lunch, I made pizza, enough to feed an army.

Though I was sure bikers would get through it all. My eyes kept drifting out the kitchen window to where the shed was. The men stayed in there doing whatever they were doing. Still, eager for a chance to see Kalen, I kept watching while cooking.

After all the pizzas were ready, I went to the side door to call out, "Lunch time." And then headed back to dish up Koda's before it all disappeared. My nerves kicked up when I heard the door open and men stomping in. Turning from my seat in front of Koda's high chair, I smiled in greeting to all.

"Looks good, babe," the one who helped me with the tray earlier said with an easy grin.

"Thanks. I wasn't sure what you all liked, so I hope you'll find one at least with something you eat."

"We'd eat just about anything, sunshine." Kalen winked. "Babe, that there is Knife, Muff, Dallas, and Beast."

Muff offered a salute, Beast a chin lift, and Dallas a head nod.

"Hi, all. Thank you for coming to help. I hope it didn't put anyone out."

"How come you're moving in, darlin'?" Muff asked.

"Um." Nervousness and embarrassment flipped my stomach.

"She's in between places," Kalen said before he shoved

a bit of pizza in his mouth. I met his eyes and smiled my gratitude for not telling them my story.

"Too bad you don't live in Caroline Springs. I would'a had you at my place, in my house and bed," Knife stated. My face went to raging heat in seconds, quickly running down my neck also.

"Knife," Kalen clipped in a rough tone.

"If she cooked like this all the time, I'd give it a try as well." Dallas grunted, taking another slice of quickly disappearing pizza.

"If she looked like that every day and couldn't cook, I'd have her in mine," Muff said. My cool hand went to cover my cheeks. Koda, finished with his food, started babbling about something and playing with his truck.

The only one who didn't say anything was Beast. Though when I looked at him, he winked at me. I quickly averted my gaze and heard a chuckle from all.

All except Kalen, who said acidly, "Jesus Christ, brothers."

When the front door opened and Judy called out, "I'm here," I sighed in relief. She came into the kitchen, smiled, and greeted everyone. She then made her way to my only escape. She took Koda from the high chair and cooed at him. "How long until you finish up?" Her eyes went to her son.

"'Bout an hour."

"Cool." She looked to me and said, "You're gonna love it. Best feeling in the world."

Confused, I asked quietly, "What?"

"Hadn't told her yet, Mum."

"Told me what?" I asked, looking to Kalen and standing from my seat.

"Gonna ride out with my brothers for a while. You're on the back of my bike."

"I'm sorry?" I whispered.

Kalen smirked, rolled his eyes and said, "You. Back of my bike in an hour."

I was stunned speechless. Kalen wanted to take me for a ride on his bike. In front of his brothers, with his brothers riding with us, around us. Did Kalen realise I would have to hold onto him, so I didn't get my brain squished on the pavement?

Hugging Kalen.

Holding Kalen.

Oh. My. God.

I fisted my trembling hands. My eyes went low, and heat hit my cheeks once again. Wow, I couldn't seem to get my blushes under control around these people. That and the fact I seemed to turn red quite a bit when Kalen came to mind.

"Sunshine?"

Looking up, I mumbled, "Hmm?"

"You in?"

"She's in," Judy announced. "Now go and get the shit done so you can go."

Kalen gave me a look I didn't understand before he followed the rest of his brothers out of the house.

Once the side door closed, I spun to Judy. Laughing at my expression, she pulled me into a side hug and said, "Why do you look so worried?"

"Does Kalen understand I've never been on a motorbike before?" That my arms would be wrapped around him?

"He can tell, like we all can. You look a little green around the gills." She laughed. "Don't worry. He's a brilliant rider. They all are." She smiled. "Oh, by the way, I have some of my clothes that don't fit me anymore in the car. They'd be perfect for you, though. There're some jeans in there. Why don't you go out and grab them while I spend time with my grandbaby."

With my chin out and up, I asked, "Did Kalen tell you about how few clothes I have?"

Her smirk told me he had, though she replied, "No, why would he do that? I was just having a clean out before I head away."

Grumbling under by breath, I headed out to Judy's car and grabbed the bags from the back seat. Really, I shouldn't complain. It was sweet he'd rang his Mum.

Very sweet in fact.

As I changed in the bathroom into jeans, a smile lit my

face. A silly smile. My stomach churned from the giddiness sweeping through me. Riding on Kalen's bike with him… I couldn't wait. In fact, I found myself skipping from the bathroom and down the hall.

"They fit perfectly," Judy commented as I came to a stop in the living room.

"I'm just going to clean the kitchen while I wait. Are you okay with Koda?"

She scoffed. "Of course."

It turned out to be an hour and a half before the men came back inside. Judy was in Koda's room putting him down for his nap. I sprung up from the couch and stood, with my hands clasped in front of me.

Kalen was the first to enter the living room, and I sucked in a hiss. He looked handsome in a rough biker looking way, wearing his biker vest. His eyes raked over me before he nodded and gave me a wink. Those winks were driving the lower half of my body crazy.

"You ready?"

"Yes." I grinned. "Though, I have to admit, I'm a bit nervous. I've never been on a bike before." Or had my hands on your waist, or been pressed close to you.

"You're a virgin." Knife laughed. "Man, let me take her on the back. I have the need to break her in."

Kalen's hand came out, and the slap to the back of Knife's head seemed to echo in the room. "Fuckin' enough." With a nod, he gestured to the door. The brothers, understanding any movement or grunt or chin lift, filed out of the house through the front door. Kalen looked back to me and said, "They can sometimes be dicks, but don't let it get to you."

Shaking my head, I said, "I won't."

"Good," he said and then went into the kitchen for something, coming back with a helmet. "I don't have a spare one right now. You can use mine."

He didn't have a spare one *right now.*

Right now.

Did that mean he was going to be getting one for me?

What was going on here?

"But, what about you? You need to be safe as well."

He smiled and pulled a piece of cloth from his back pocket. He tied it around the top of his head. It was a bandana, and he looked amazing in one.

What would his beard feel like on my body?

Oh, God. Where did that thought come from?

"Ready?"

"Yes," I answered breathily.

Mind still thinking about his beard, I watched his lips twitch, lips I could see clearly because he kept his beard trimmed nicely. I lowered my gaze, taking a calming breath. I had no idea how I would survive pressed against him and not turn into a puddle of goo.

He started for the door, and I followed quietly. The sun was still shining down on us. No dark clouds marred the sky. His brothers were already astride their rides waiting for us. Kalen stopped beside his and flung his leg over.

"You need to put the helmet on first, sunshine." He smiled. I fumbled with it and placed it on my head. I tried doing up the straps, but I couldn't work it out. Were they freaking childproof? Or did you need to take a course on it? Chuckling, Kalen demanded, "Come here, woman." I stepped up to him. His warm hands went to the straps and too soon, he had it done up. "Throw your leg over and slide on, Mena."

"Um, okay." I nodded yet stood frozen. I wasn't sure I was ready for a ride.

My decision was taken from me when suddenly a large presence was behind me, Dallas. I let out a squeak of surprise when he picked me up and sat me straight in behind Kalen. Then, to my utter embarrassment, he placed his hand on my butt and pushed me forward, so my crotch pressed against Kalen's lower back and butt. Finally, if that wasn't bad enough, he took my arm and wound it around Kalen's waist. I quickly did the other one and gripped them to Kalen's leather vest.

"Done. Now let's ride," Dallas barked.

All the men, even Kalen, threw their heads back and laughed. Of course, I watched Kalen. When he'd calmed down, he looked over his shoulder and asked, "You good?"

"I'm afraid to move in case Dallas comes back to rearrange me."

He chuckled. "You're good." He slid his mirrored sunglasses onto his nose and kicked his bike to start.

Judy was right. I freaking loved riding. Holding Kalen close wasn't the only fact I loved so much about riding. It was being surrounded by his brothers, feeling safe with them all. It was the wind, the smell, and the sound. It was everything combined.

After an hour-long ride, we had a quick coffee in town before Kalen's brothers headed back to Caroline Springs. Feeling in the best mood, I made them all suffer through a hug and thanks for coming to help. Though, the only ones who really suffered were Dallas and Beast. Knife went to feel my butt up until I smacked his hand away and glared. He was a tease and nothing else.

I didn't want the afternoon to end, but all too soon, we were pulling up out the front of the house. I climbed off, and while I took off my helmet, Kalen hopped off, and then I passed it over to him. He placed it on the seat behind him.

"Wanna see your room?"

Smiling, I said excitedly, "Yes, please. But, will Judy mind us being a bit longer?"

He snorted. "Nope."

We walked across the lawn. I trailed a bit because my legs were a little like jelly. They weren't used to sitting on a Harley. Kalen already had the door open and stepping in by the time I was there.

Gasping, my hands went to my chest. Then I slid one to cover my mouth because my bottom lip trembled. Tears filled my eyes and my heart beat at a frantic, excited pace.

It was wonderful.

No, it was amazing.

Beautiful and special.

Kalen had done this for me. Having someone give so freely meant more to me than anything I had experienced in life.

There was a bed in the far back, and next to it were some drawers. On the other side was a nightstand with a lamp. In the space at the end of the bed, sat a couch. Opposite it was the TV and stand. A little kitchenette was to the left of the room. It had a bar fridge and a small two-seater table. The room seemed warm. My eye landed on the heater to the right of the room. Everything was perfect.

"There's a toilet room with sink to the side of the bed, but it don't have a shower, so you'll have to use the one inside. We cleaned it up as much as we could. Some stuff was already in here. The rest we got in from my place in Caroline Springs."

"Kalen… it's fantastic. No, more than that, but I can't

think of the right word to use." My voice hitched. "I, you, I mean… I don't know what to say."

"Nothing is needed to be said, Mena. Glad you like it. I'll leave you to it." He started for the door, only to face me again and say, "There're some things in the fridge already. I asked Mum to fill it. But, did you want to grab something inside for dinner?"

"Thank you, but do you mind if I stay out here? Unless you would like me to cook something for you and Koda?"

"All good. Koda would have eaten with Mum, so I'll just grab a sandwich or something. See you in the morning, Mena." He turned to the door again, but I called his name and rushed at him. I had to hug him. The day had been perfect. I had to hold him and show him how much it meant. Before he could wrap his arms around me, if that was his intention, I moved back.

Smiling up at him with tears in my eyes, I said, "Thank you again. So much, Kalen, thank you."

He winked. My heart winked with him. "No problem," he said gruffly before he walked out, closing the door behind him.

TWO WEEKS LATER

DIVE

She wouldn't eat dinner with us. She'd make it, and then, once I got home, she'd take off out to her shed. I'd asked, but she'd said she had her meal already. Shit, I found myself hoping for the last two weeks she'd stay, keep me company, and eat with us. Even after Koda was in bed, I stood at the kitchen window looking out to the light in the shed and wondered what she was up to. Mum was away on another trip, so I knew she wasn't getting any food from her. Then again, Mena was more than capable to go into town to buy her food in her car during the day, after I'd given her keys back. I trusted she wouldn't up and leave. She loved Koda too much to leave him.

What did she think of me, though?

I didn't have a fucking clue.

I wanted… no, I needed to get to know her.

Fucking hell, why didn't she want to spend time with me at night?

Fed up with pining for her company, I opened the door and took the steps it took to get to her door in a quick stride and knocked.

The moment it opened, I barked, "You eaten?" Then, fuck me, my eyes slid over her and I had to hide my smile when I saw her dressed in Big Bird PJs and slippers that had the head of Big Bird as well. They looked fucked-up for a thirty-year-old to wear them, but still, she looked goddamn cute.

"Um, yes?"

What in the fuck? Why was she answering in a question?

With a hand on her belly, I pressed forward, and she moved aside. I stalked to the kitchen and opened the fridge. Milk, cheese, and some vegetables stared back at me. I picked up the last carrot, and it flopped to the side. Growling low, I threw it in the sink and moved to the small cupboard and opened it. Fucking cups of soup and noodles.

Spinning to face her, I took in her heated cheeks and wide eyes. "This is what you ate for dinner?"

Her eyes narrowed, her chin jutted out and up, and she hissed, "Yes."

"This isn't enough, Mena."

"It's done me fine for nine months, Kalen."

"I want you in the house every night to eat with us."

"No." Her hands went to her hips, an action I was becoming familiar with, and her upper body edged forward.

"Why in the fuck not? Do you hate being around me so much you refuse to be in the house when Koda isn't around? I haven't been a prick to you for a long time, Mena. You don't have to hide from me now."

Her eyes widened. "No, God no, Kalen." Her sass was gone. Her bottom lip trembled. A lip I wanted to take between my goddamn teeth and suck on. "You've already done so much for me. I couldn't ask for more." She sighed. "I don't want to become a nuisance."

Groaning, I scrubbed a hand over my face and stepped close to her. "Sunshine, you'd never be a nuisance. And Jesus, it's only food. Food you fuckin' cook anyway for me and Koda, so why not make a little extra for yourself. You eat lunch outta my cupboard already, so what's another meal that I don't give two fucks about.

And hell, you eat like a mouse anyway. Just… do it for me?"

With the back of her hand, she wiped the tears that escaped. Hell, she was even stunning when she cried. Most woman got all snotty, red-eyed, and crazy looking. She didn't.

"Okay," she whispered to the floor and then looked up at me. "Thank you."

Rolling my eyes, I smiled and said, "Woman, don't thank me. Koda and I love your cooking. If anything, I'm being selfish for that reason alone." She giggled. "Have you eaten already?"

"Well, yes."

"Come in for a snack then." I didn't want to lose her company just yet.

"I'd like that. But I should get changed first."

"Sunshine, it's right out there." I gestured with my thumb outside. "I don't think anyone would see you in your pyjamas, and I promise to keep your fascination with Big Bird a secret." Her cheeks pinked and my dick twitched, like it did every time I saw colour touch her face. I chuckled and then reached out for her hand. Dragging her out of the room, I closed her door and led her to the house. Once inside, I let go of her hand and grabbed the baby monitor out of the back of my jeans and placed it on the table.

"What do you feel like?" I asked, heading for the cupboards.

"Anything, thanks." She took a seat at the kitchen table while I got out some bread and vegemite, then the butter from the fridge. "I'm not much of a cook, but I can do a mean vegemite sandwich with cheese."

She smiled. "Sounds great to me."

We were silent until I placed her sandwich down in front of her with a bottle of beer. "You do drink this, right? You weren't just being polite last time and just had it for the sake of it?"

"No, I really do drink it. Though, it may go straight to my head."

"Don't worry, I'll get you to bed if it does."

Not sure which bed it would be, though.

Fuck. No, I can't be thinkin' that shit.

"So, um, can I ask you something?"

"Yeah." I nodded and watched her take a bite of her sandwich, chew, and then swallow. Hell, was I staring too much? I took a pull of beer and waited while munching on my own.

"How did you become a biker?"

Sitting back in the seat, I shrugged. "My dad used to be one. Guess it was born and bred in me. Though, I hated the club he was with. Rough, mean fuckers who didn't give a shit about anything. They sold powder, pussy, and guns. Knew I'd never want to be a part of that when I saw the shit my mum went through worrying about the dick."

"Hawks doesn't deal with any of that?" she asked hesitantly. It was my fault for her thinking I would say shit about myself. I'd never broached the subject of me and wanted nothing to do with her either. But shit had changed.

"Fuck no. Which is what I admire about them. Some of my brothers and I used to live in Ballarat where the main charter is. Talon is the president for all charters. When he got in charge, he stopped all illegal bullshit happening in the club. He wanted it clean, so all brothers could breathe easy. Now we own some strip clubs and mechanical places we help out in. Then, Talon sent me and Dodge down to Caroline Springs to help Pick and Billy out when they were goin' through some shit with Josie. Now it's home for us."

"You all seem really close," she commented before taking her last bite.

"Yeah." I smiled. "It's the way things are in the club. Fuckin' proud to call them all my brothers. They know I'd be there for them for anything, and I know it's the same for me. Like today, they're only a phone call away, and they'll willingly drop shit to help me out. Like I'd do for them."

"How come, um, why did you move from them?"

Shit. Wasn't sure I was ready for that conversation.

"One day, I'll head back. My life *is* in Caroline Springs. For now, I just needed time for me and Koda." Taking the last gulp of beer, I leaned forward and told her, "Koda's mum…" Fuck. "She died giving birth to him." She gasped. Her hand went up to cover her mouth. "Thing was, I didn't know she was pregnant until the day she gave birth to him."

"W-why?"

Picking at the label on the bottle, I said, "She was sick. I knew she was tired all the time, but I thought it was stress from uni. She didn't tell anyone she had a tumour around her heart and brain. She got pregnant with my kid because she wanted to leave something of her behind."

"You loved her," she whispered. How she knew it, I had no clue. Maybe she read it on my face.

Nodding, I said, "Yeah, I did. I had so many months with her, but I was chasing her way before that. Then she decided she wanted to protect me from seeing her sick all the time, so she left with my kid in her."

"So you missed out on Koda growing in her and being able to take care of her when you loved her and would have done anything for her."

Well, fuck. She got it in one.

"That's it. I was pissed for so long and mourning her at the same time. I took a lot of shit out on you, and I'm fuckin' sorry for it."

She smiled shyly and shrugged. "I knew something was battling inside of you. I just thought you hated me."

A snort escaped, and then I said, "I doubt anyone could hate you."

"Oh, there have been a few."

Getting up, I went to the fridge to grab another beer. Turning, I asked, "Want another?"

She lifted hers, shaking it. "I still have half, and besides, I have to be up and ready early for Koda. Um, how are you liking work?"

"S'okay," I said, sitting down. "Keeps me busy. For a while there, I hated it because it kept me away from Koda, but I realised I was becoming too protective of him."

"Worried something would happen to him as well?"

"Yeah, I was. To the point, I was looking up home-schooling him. Wouldn't surprise me if I tried to get one of those bubbles for him to live in." She giggled. "No joke, even a sumo suit was a possibility. Then, I wouldn't want him picked on, so I'd have to get one for myself and beat any fucker who said shit."

She burst out laughing. "Stop," she begged. "I keep picturing it," she managed through her giggles. After she had calmed down, she told me, "I'm glad you're protective, but I'm also glad you got a job, or I wouldn't have met either of you—and, um, Judy is amazing. So easy to get along with." She blushed. "Anyway, um, I've been wondering for a while, and even your friends wouldn't tell me, but why Dive for a biker name?"

Fuck me sideways and with a cactus.

Jesus, I felt my cheeks heat.

Of course she saw it, even around my beard, because she said, "It can't be that bad."

"Sunshine, it's best you don't ask right now."

She sat straight and clapped her hands. "No way, I need to know now."

Groaning, I sank down lower in my seat and begged, "Please don't ask me."

"Oh, my God. How can Dive be so bad? I don't get it unless you like to dive into trouble?" I shook my head. "Dive into food?" Another headshake. "Alcohol?" Shake. "Wait, it has to be something biker, right?" I shrugged. She tapped her chin while she thought about it. "Riding, you like to dive into riding or fixing bikes?"

"Sunshine, for the love of Harleys, please do not ask me."

She giggled. Maybe I shouldn't have given her that beer. "No, I'll get it right."

"You won't," I stated.

"How long have you been a biker?"

"Since I was sixteen, but with Hawks for only fifteen years."

"Did you have your club name at sixteen?"

"Shit," I grumbled low.

Her hand slapped the table. "It must be something juvenile."

"Think it's time for you to head back," I said, standing from my seat.

She jumped up. "It is something juvenile. This is precious. Oh, my God, what could it be that you would be embarrassed about?"

Hell, I'd never, not once, been embarrassed about my club name. In fact, I thought it the bomb, loved sharing it with all women. Until sunshine. I didn't want her to know what a dirty fucker I was.

Stepping close, I watched as she slowly looked up into my eyes. "Woman, you need to leave this alone."

Her smile was huge. "I can't. It's too juicy not to know." She licked her lips. My eyes followed, and I wondered what she tasted like.

"Christ, all right, sunshine. I'll tell you, but I'll walk you back first." Taking her hand again, because any chance I could get, I felt like I needed to touch her. I took her out of the house and opened her door to the shed where I shifted her in, turned her, and said, "The name Dive." She nodded. "I claimed it because I love to dive into pussy with my mouth." With a hand on her belly, I gently shoved her back and closed her door. Still, I didn't miss her eyes widen, only to sink lower and fill with heat. Nor did I miss the gasp that fell softly from her lips.

Fucking hell. My cock, already a semi from being

around her, grew rock-hard at the thought of her playing with herself while picturing me diving into her pussy.

My steps back to the house were fast. Temptation beat at me to turn back around to find out if my image could come true. Fuck, the image was too much.

CHAPTER SIXTEEN

TWO MONTHS LATER

MENA

Ever since Kalen had said those words to me, that he liked, no he *loved* to dive into pussy with his mouth, my panties had been wet. And, nearly every night, I touched myself picturing it was Kalen caressing me. Kalen with his mouth down there on me, and Kalen slipping himself deep inside of me.

My raw, lust-filled emotions were driving me insane. I couldn't get his words out of my head. So much so, every time I saw him, my dang cheeks would colour, and he knew why as well. In fact, he seemed to enjoy seeing my cheeks pink because then he would give me a cocky smirk or wink.

Despite the sexual tension between us, we never made a move to the next step. I'd considered it plenty of times, but I was worried he was still in love with Koda's mum. I worried I would lose what I had if I tried anything. My life was finally feeling safe and happiness had become a regular fixture. I wasn't ready to take a risk and ruin it all for me to have sex with Kalen. There was also a chance that if we did, things could go down the drain after. I couldn't handle that happening.

Living in the shed helped a lot. It was that little bit of extra space between us I needed. Though, we still ate dinner together every night, and Kalen and I talked for an hour or so after Koda was in bed. Those talks were near torture for me. I wasn't sure if it was just me feeling it, but I had to fight with myself each night from jumping him. There seemed to be extra heat in our glances, the extra lingering of touches if we accidently brushed against each other.

What also didn't help was the few mornings I got into the house early and caught Kalen coming from the bathroom in nothing but a towel. He didn't notice me each time. A stray thought had hoped he would because I wanted to see where it would go... no doubt with me blushing and running from the house. Though, in my fantasy, he would drop the towel and tell me to meet him in his room because he wanted to show me what a real man could do with his body.

So I stopped going in earlier to prevent my wayward crazy fantasy.

I had to stay strong.

There was too much to risk.

Judy had been on a trip, came back, and was away again on another. This one was a short one, and she'd be back in two days. Each time she left, I missed her. She was a wonderful mother and grandmother, and I had come to love her like a mother too.

Koda was growing so much. He wasn't quite walking yet, though his crawl along the floor was faster than when he'd started, and he liked to pull himself up on everything he could. Even one of the long skirts Judy had given me. The only problem with that was it was loose, so when he went to pull himself up, the skirt came down instead. Thank God, no one was around to see it beside Koda. He thought it was the funniest thing and tried to do it many times that afternoon.

Koda was now saying three more words: ball, ta (for thank you), and Nena, for my name. Of course, when he said it the first time, I used some of my saved money, and went out and bought him some large Lego blocks.

Staying where I was had helped me so much. My debt was growing smaller each week. I was saving, even if it was a tiny amount. The only problem was with the extra food I was eating, I was gaining weight. Still, there was no way I would complain. It was but a passing thought because I was safe, warm, never hungry, and I was cared for.

It was a Saturday. Kalen had given me the morning off, not that I usually worked or got paid for weekends, but I loved cooking for them. Though Kalen said he would handle breakfast, so I could have a sleep in. I didn't of course. My body clock seemed to like torturing me and waking me at six thirty every morning. Didn't matter, though; I had my morning planned out. I'd decided to treat myself. I even bought discounted nail polish, a facemask, and a waxing kit. All of it was a steal at five dollars. Just finishing the cobalt blue nail polish on my fingers and toes while I waited for my facemask and now nails to dry, I went to the kitchenette to make myself a coffee. `

The next part wasn't something I had ever done, so my nerves were fierce. Since it was too early for a stiff drink, I grabbed out the chocolate Judy had supplied me with and ate some. After checking my nails were dry, I washed my face and sat on the edge of my bed with nothing but a long, loose tee on.

Gulping, I lifted my tee and spread my legs. Looking at the wax paper, I warmed it between my hands like it read on the box and then pulled the backing off. Before I could chicken out, I placed it on my mound Then I did that over and over with another four strips, thinking if I could yank it all out in one go, the pain would be over in seconds.

I was wrong.

It was all a stupid idea.

What in the heck had I been thinking?

Yes, let me pamper myself by ripping out my pubes.

Brilliant idea.

Taking a hold of one end, I tried to pull it away. Instead, I whimpered, and tears filled my eyes. Curling in a ball and crying would be a great option. Ignorance was bliss, right? Except when I went to move, the strips pulled at my pubes causing me to cry out in pain.

Then there was a knock at my door.

With wide eyes, I looked, searched for anything... only, I didn't know what the heck I was searching for because there was nothing that could help me in that situation.

"Mena?" a woman's voice called. A voice I knew well since she called nearly every week to see how I was going. A woman who was amazingly friendly and made me feel like I was a part of her friends' circle.

"Um." I needed help. As embarrassing as it was, I needed some help and quick. "Come in."

The door opened, and Low stepped in talking, "Hey, girlfriend. Dodge, the kids, and I thought we'd pop up for a surprise visit. Then Mattie and Julian with their gorgeous girl were staying in town last night seeing Josie, and they decided they'd come for the trip up also. You have to come inside. Koda and Aeila look so cute together." She laughed. "Julian reckons she'll be a cougar like him. Not that she's much older than Koda." She stopped and studied me. "Girl, what's going on?"

"I've done something really stupid."

She glanced around the room. "What?"

"Um, I'm stuck."

She threw her hands up in the air. "Mena, spell it out for me. How are you stuck?"

"I, ah, I thought with the morning to myself I would do some pampering." Low gestured with her hand in a circular motion for me to continue. "I painted my nails, did a facemask and… um, tried waxing."

Her eyes widened. Her hand covered her mouth. "No," she whispered. Tears filled my eyes again, and I nodded. "Oh, honey. Down there?" I nodded again. "Oh no. Hang on one second." She rushed from the room. I wasn't sure where she was going or what she was doing. At least it didn't take her long to get back. The door opened and she came in, but… holy heckle, she'd brought a tall, gorgeous man with her.

"Hey, sugar plum, I'm Julian. Low said you were in a situation." He smiled calmly and shut the door behind him. Not a second ticked by when there was a knock on the door.

"Mena, you okay in there?"

Kill me now. It was Kalen.

"Yep, uh, all good. Thank you. I'll be out soon to prepare lunch," I called.

"Are you sure?"

"Yes," I squeaked.

"Dude, give us a few, and we'll be out," Low yelled. Then she went to the door to check. I heard her mumbling something, and then she closed the door and came to stand beside Julian. She rubbed her hands together and said, "Right, let's get this situation under control."

Glaring, I asked, "What are you going to do?"

"Finish the job."

"No." I gasped. "Can't we just pour something on it to get it off?"

She shook her head. "Won't work like that."

Glancing at Julian, I said in alarm, "Maybe I could do it on my own."

"Babe, you would have already done it if you could."

"You-hoo, does anyone want to tell me what the situation is and how I can help?" Julian asked. His hands went to his slim denim-clad hips.

Low went on her tippy toes and whispered into his ear.

When she stood back on her feet, Julian turned to me and said, "Sweetness, do not fret. Before I became a masseuse, I did a course in beauty, and waxing was a part of it." He took his jacket off and placed it on the couch. Then he came towards me while rolling up his sleeves on his shirt.

"Um, I don't think… I'm not sure. You're a guy. I don't know if I feel comfortable with this." I went to scoot back on the bed, only to wince when the strips pulled again.

"Doll face, even if I'm a guy, I'm 100 percent gay. My hot dog won't even get hard over staring at your bun. It's all good. I know what I'm doing. Low, come and hold her hand."

"Why will she need to hold my hand?" I gasped.

He stopped next to the bed, sighed, then sat beside me, patting my thigh. "I'm not going to beat around the bush, ha, get it, bush, your bush."

"Julian," Low snapped.

"Sorry, getting off track. By now, my guess is you already know it's going to hurt like a motherfucker. Excuse the language. You squeeze down on Low's hand for support."

Sweat formed all over my body. My heart wanted to jump out of my butt and cry in the corner, and my vagina was whimpering for the pain it was about to go through.

"Open up," Julian said like it was nothing, like he wasn't climbing onto the bed on his knees and trying to pry my legs apart.

"I can't do this."

"You can," Low replied. "We're here for you. Just breathe through it."

"I'm not having a freaking baby. My pubic hairs are about to be ripped out of my body." Groaning, I lay back on the bed, my hand over my face. "What was I thinking?"

"Doing a clean-up before Dive gets down there?" Julian offered.

My head snapped up. "What? No! It's not like that."

"Uh-huh," Low muttered, then giggled. "Come on, before Dive comes to check we aren't corrupting you in any way. Let's get this shit done." She tapped my shin.

"I'm so embarrassed." But I braved it. I couldn't keep the wax on there; it could rot on my mound and then it would be worse. Sighing, I closed my eyes, covered my face with one hand and I spread my legs in front of a man I didn't know. The other hand, I reached out blindly. Low took hold.

"Oh, shit," Julian whispered.

"What?" I yelled. My eyes sprung open to look down at him. "Sugar, that's a lot of wax strips. What were you thinking? That you had a beast down there to tame?"

No," I cried. "I thought if I laid them all on I could rip them all off at the same time. I've never done this before."

Julian and Low shared a concerned look before Julian leaned in, met my eyes, and said, "Brace."

Gripping Low's hand hard, I braced, but I was never prepared for the pain. It felt like he was tearing my soul from my body.

"Fuck!" I screamed. My whole body tingled. More sweat pooled over my body. "I-Is that it? Are we done? Please tell me we're done."

"Sorry, sweetgums, that was only the first one."

"No, no, no."

"Brace," Julian said.

"No!" I screamed as he tore another part of my soul away. My poor, poor vagina was crying and burning like it had been dipped in hell. Then Julian did it again and again. *Rip, rip, rip.*

"A-are we done?" I puffed.

"One more. You're doing such a good job," Julian commented, and I wanted to punch him in the face for it. He wasn't the one with a burning vagina.

"Speak for yourself," Low snapped. "I have no feeling in my hand left."

"S-sorry…" *Rip.* "Fuck me!"

To my utter mortification, my door was thrown open so hard it hit the wall.

"What the fuck?" Kalen boomed into the room.

Kill me now. Strike me down and take me to hell to join with my vagina so we can become one again.

"Julian, do you want to tell me why you're bent between Mena's legs before Dive kills you?" the one man

I hadn't met asked, who I presumed was Mattie, Julian's partner.

"And, little bird, tell me why you're watching," Dodge asked, and I could hear the humour in his voice.

"For moral support," Low said as if her words explained it all.

"Get the fuck off the bed and outta here… what, you… Jesus, Julian, only you would get to…" Kalen trailed off.

Low quickly stood, picked up a blanket, and threw it over my lower half. My lower half that was still irritated and wailing in pain.

Julian slowly moved off the bed and stood. Then he turned back and leaned down to me and whispered, "You need to gently wash the area and then apply aloe cream. Sorry, pet, you're going to be sore for a little bit."

Nodding, I said, "Thank you."

"Pleasure." He smiled.

"What was a fuckin' pleasure?"

"Brother, I think we need to leave them to it."

"Screw that, I want to know what happened."

Julian started for them. As he passed Kalen, he patted his shoulder and said, "Let Mena get cleaned up, and she can tell you if she wants. But, I'll tell you now her curtains match her drapes." I gasped. Kalen's jaw dropped open and he spun, heading after Julian. He would have grabbed him if Dodge hadn't held him back.

"I'm sure there's a perfect explanation for it. Cool it down, brother."

"There is," Low called from where she still stood beside the door.

I gasped. "Low."

My face was bright red. Never had I felt so humiliated in my whole life. Not even when I was living out of my car, and one time had to beg for money.

"Okay, get out." Low clapped. Everyone left, and I knew right then, I was about to become a hermit, never leaving my room or facing anyone ever again.

Well, I would have if I hadn't needed a shower and aloe vera.

CHAPTER SEVENTEEN

MENA

I went through the laundry back door to grab some clean underwear from the dryer I didn't get to fold from the day before. It wasn't like I was hiding from anyone. At least, that was what I told myself.

Taking the clothes from the dryer, I realised I was missing my favourite pair, the only red lacy ones I owned. I swore I placed them in the washing with Koda and Kalen's stuff. My face heated when my hands grabbed a pair of Kalen's boxers from the dryer. His penis had been rubbing against them. I quickly put them in the basket. I didn't want anyone catching me rubbing them against my face like I felt like doing, which was weird.

Putting my missing panties out of my mind, I grabbed another pair and snuck down the hall to the bathroom. After locking the door, I pulled my tee off and looked down between my legs. My poor, poor vagina was bright red. God, it looked like it was red in anger. I was sure if it could speak, it would be cursing me like a sailor.

Don't worry, I'll make you feel better. I reassured it as I turned on the shower. I couldn't make it too hot, which I quickly discovered, after yelping in pain.

If there were a day I could rewind and do all over again, it would definitely be that day. The only other person who'd seen my privates was Mark, and now there was Julian and Low. God, Kalen, Dodge, and Mattie nearly got a good look as well. Well, they would have if they'd come in earlier.

Just thinking of it, I wanted to dig myself a hole and have someone bury me in it. I wanted to run back to my room, pack, and leave town. However, I couldn't. Even if I really, really wanted to.

Towelling down, I gently patted my angry mound and then rubbed the cool aloe vera into it. Well, not rubbed, more like tapped. My eyes drifted to my clothes. I should have thought it through more. I had jeans and a tee. My skin still stung, and I just knew clothing would irritate it more.

"Mena?" came from outside the door.

Walking to it, I opened it slightly and looked to a cringing Low. "How's it going?"

"I think I need a dress. Stupidly, I'd grabbed jeans. I don't think my, *huh-hum,* would enjoy the closeness of clothes just yet."

She nodded. "I'll run out and grab one for you."

"Thank you."

"You know, this brings our friendship that little bit closer. I've seen your twat after all. Don't tell Lucia. She'll try and flash me hers."

A laugh escaped me as she walked away. Low had many times told me all about her friend Lucia. I thought Low had an out-there personality, but the stories I'd heard of her friend told me she was way worse than Low. One day, I hoped to meet her and get to know Josie and Nary better. She'd told me all about her ordeal. I was gobsmacked she'd been through so much and yet, she was still full of life. She'd explained the reason why she was together was because of Dodge. He made her feel safe.

I mentioned I felt the same in a way. Nothing like her horrific story, but I told her about my life and how I'd come to Kalen's and how he'd saved me from living a life in my car. That was when she'd asked if I liked him.

"Girl, I know he was an arse to you at the start, but I can hear from your voice it's changed now. Do you like him?"

It seemed my pause was answer enough to her.

She whispered in the phone, "I think you would be good for him."

"Low," I said softly. "It can't—"

"Never say can't. Just go with the flow, woman, and don't let anything foolish stop you from having what you want."

"He doesn't—"

"Mena, just go with the flow."

"Okay, honey. I will."

Low was generous to offer me her friendship. In life, I hadn't had many. Mark had been my everything and all I'd needed. But talking to Low like that and knowing she wouldn't say anything to Kalen, it was special, new, and I loved it.

A knock came and I opened the door again and smiled at Low as she handed over my yellow sundress. She winked and said, "I'm gonna get a start on lunch. Come help me when you get out of there."

My heart jogged faster. "I don't know if—"

"Woman. Come help me. It'll be fine, and if it's not, I'll hurt them myself for you."

"Promise?" I smiled.

Getting dressed was an effort all on its own. My movement was restricted from the soreness. My vagina nearly revolted when I placed panties over it, but I wasn't wearing a dress and no panties in case I ended up flashing someone while getting lunch. Knowing my luck, it could happen.

My stomach dropped to my feet. My face and neck heated from just thinking of walking out in the kitchen. Julian had been down there.

Down there and I had to face not only him but his partner as well.

God, and Kalen knew he'd been looking at me down there. So did Dodge.

I couldn't do it.

But I had to.

Strong. I had to be strong.

Even though my hands shook, and I felt like I was going to throw my precious chocolate up, I grabbed the door handle, twisted it, and started down the hall.

My body trembled. Sweat formed under my arms. There was no doubt I'd need another shower soon. Still, I kept my stiff body moving and stepped into the living room where I found Tex and Rommy. There was also a gorgeous dark-headed little girl, who looked to be a couple of months older than Koda. They were all on the floor playing until Rommy looked up and noticed me. She bounced up and came to stand in front of me.

"Hi, Mena, wanna come play?"

"I'd love to, but maybe later. I have to help Low in the kitchen with lunch." I touched a hand to her head and smiled down at her. Seeing Tex looking, I sent him a wave and he gave me a chin lift back. Exactly like his uncle.

Before I chickened out, I walked past the window that connected the kitchen and living room and went straight into the kitchen, to the bench where Low was standing while all the men sat at the table.

"You okay, sweetness?" Julian asked.

"Fine, thank you," I said to the bench. My cheeks were so hot, not nearly as hot as my lower area, but still, if I didn't stop flushing soon, I was worried I'd pass out. Braving the world, okay room, I looked up to the table, met Mattie and Julian's gaze, and said, "Your daughter is beautiful."

Mattie smiled and said, "Thanks, we think so too."

Risking a glance at Kalen, I had to grip the bench hard to hold me up. His gaze was on me, only it was low. Oh, God, they'd told him. Stupidly, I thought they wouldn't say anything. Then again, they probably hadn't, but it was a damn good guess what had been going on. Especially since Julian was gay and wouldn't usually be caught dead in that area.

Inhaling deeply, I spat out, "I'm sorry you had to find Julian in that position. I don't know what I was thinking. But I wish we could *all* forget it even happened."

Mattie chuckled. "Don't worry about it, Mena. I really never know what Julian will get up to next, so I just go with it."

"He also knows I'm only interested in his lovin' and

no one else's. Like I said, I'm a hot dog man, not a bun one or I could say—"

"We get it," Dodge griped. "Mena." He grunted, and I looked at him. "Don't stress. The image of my little bird next to you with your legs spread—" It all happened so fast. He shut up when a hand palmed his face and in the next second, he was forced back, his chair going with him, and they both crashed to the floor. He groaned and slowly rolled to the side, rubbing the back of his head.

"Not another fuckin' word," Kalen snarled down at him.

"Come on, brother." Dodge smirked. How could he find that funny? "It's about time I told everyone some embarrassing shit you used to do all the time."

"Oh, he did stupid shit." Low giggled. "Like the first time you met Lucia—"

"Low, no," Kalen growled in warning. My head went back and forth between them.

She hid her laugh behind her hand and went back to buttering some bread. "Suppose you have grown up a bit." She smirked and then winked. "So don't piss me off and manhandle my man, and I'll keep all the stuff you did a secret."

Kalen rolled his eyes at her, and then he glanced at me and smiled. "You gonna get some lunch goin' before we all fade away to nothing?"

Pulling my lips between my teeth, I bit down to hide

my beaming smile. He was changing the subject. Giving me the out I wanted.

"I doubt any of you will fade away, but I will get on with it." Bumping hips with Low, I grumbled, "Men."

"Tell me about it, girl." We shared a smile and got down to lunch.

OUR VISITORS DIDN'T LEAVE until late afternoon. I wasn't sure if I could call them *our* visitors, but I did. Low was a good friend now, and besides, Julian had seen my private parts, so he instantly became a friend once he went down there.

After they had left, Kalen went into town to do a few things while I took Koda for a play and walk outside. Kalen ended up ringing later saying he was bringing fish and chips home for dinner. I was happy with that; it meant I didn't have to do anything.

When he got back, I couldn't help but feel he kept eyeing my lower area more and more. I wondered what he was thinking. There was no way I would broach the subject, so we kept to small talk until Kalen decided to go deep, just not in the way I would have like him to. Instead, he asked about Mark.

"Do you miss him?"

"Every day," I said honestly. Kalen got a look on his face I didn't understand.

"If he were still alive today, do you think you would still be with him?"

I took my time to think about it. Shrugging, I replied, "Honestly, probably. Mark had been there for me through it all, being poor, losing my parents, putting up with the terrible things kids and then teens used to do and say to me. He was my best friend. I know I did a stupid thing standing by and letting him rake up a lot of debt, but I was afraid of losing him. I was afraid if I said anything, if I acted wrong… Everything was a worry for me. I didn't, no, I couldn't lose the only person who cared about me. Who would worry if I got sick, if I failed a test?" Laughing, I added, "Even if I stubbed my toe."

"He sounds like a great guy."

"He was." Biting my bottom lip, I shyly added, "But I was never in love with him, and I felt so guilty for it." Looking to Koda, I smiled when he shoved a fistful of fish in his mouth. "It's terrible to say, and I feel guilty for saying it, but if Mark was still alive, I would have regretted not getting a chance to meet Koda… and you."

Kalen suddenly scooted back his chair and stood, facing the sink away from Koda and me. His breath was fast. His back heaved from it, and after a few moments, I knew why because he said, "I wish Simone were still alive." My stomach dropped and my hands went to it. "I wish Koda got the chance to meet her. She was a fuckin' awesome woman, but…" He faced me. "Koda wouldn't have had the chance to meet you, and neither would I. I know what guilt feels like, Mena."

He did.

He knew it as much as I did.

He cleared his throat. "I better get Koda in the bath before bed." Then he smirked with a wink. "You'd better go rest your soreness. Couldn't help but notice you wincing and walkin' funny, sunshine."

I palmed my face as it heated. "You just had to go there." Quickly, I said a goodnight to Koda with a kiss and a lame wave to Kalen. I heard his chuckle as I walked out the door.

CHAPTER EIGHTEEN

DIVE

Mentally, I gave myself a pat on the back for not jumping across the table and taking Mena there on the floor. Having Koda at the table helped. When she talked about Mark, I felt like I wanted to throw up. She loved him. It was obvious when she talked about him. However, she admitted it herself; she hadn't even been in love with him. Guilt and fear had her staying with him and with the situation she'd been in, I could see why she chose it that way.

Everything she said I paid attention. Everything she did I watched.

She was constantly occupying my mind.

God, I'd been fucking hard all day from the thought of her bare pussy.

Walking out of Koda's room, a chuckle escaped me thinking about the messed-up shit that happened. When I'd first opened her door, after hearing her scream like someone was trying to kill her, I saw red. I would have ripped and beat Julian to a bloody pulp if Low hadn't been sitting beside them. Knowing something was up helped settle me. Still, the fact that Julian got to see her sweet pussy first pissed me right the fuck off. Then when he walked by and stated her curtains matched her drapes, and I didn't get the chance to see it, I was ready to take the fucker down. Luckily, Dodge grabbed me.

What in the hell had she been thinking? Christ, she'd be sore as fuck. I hadn't been lying about noticing her wince and sit slowly or walk with a limp. Dodge and I were fighting with ourselves the whole time not to burst out laughing.

The more time I spent with Mena, the more I liked. Christ, I never thought she'd try to wax her twat and then not be able to do it. She must have been in so much pain to accept help from Low and Julian. Hell, anyone could see she was highly embarrassed about it all. Any normal person would be. Still, the way she handled it told me she had guts.

The attraction was growing more and more each day.

What I wanted was to go to her room and see the damage the waxing had done, see if there was anything, I could do to ease the pain. Shit, even my dick was jerking behind my jeans at the thought. I wanted her to spread her legs so I could get an eyeful. I wanted to kiss it better and then taste her juices.

Fuck me.

It was early, but with the thoughts I was having, I headed to my room knowing if I didn't tug one out, I'd be hard for the rest of the night.

Before I even got my door closed, I pulled off my tee and then shut the door. I went straight to the bed and lifted my pillow, staring down at what I'd stolen that morning.

Her lacy red panties.

I'd been searching through the dryer for a tee when I'd come across them. I'd snapped them up even before I thought about it. Like a druggie on a high, I'd put them to my face and sniffed, only to be disappointed when they smelled clean. Then I felt like a fucking dirty prick; still, it didn't stop me from pocketing them and taking them to my room.

They'd been on my mind all day. Picturing them against her pale flesh, imagining me slowly gliding them down her legs. That would be when I'd bring them to my nose, after she'd worn them to draw in her sweet scent.

Christ, my dick was leaking already from thinking of it.

Kicking off my boots, I undid my button on my jeans and slid them off with my boxers as well.

Was I really about to do what I was?

Jesus, yes.

Picking up her panties, I shifted the pillow back and sat on the bed, dragging my legs up as well. Bloody hell, I found myself wishing they smelt like her once again. I wanted to know her pussy scent. Fucking bet I'd enjoy it a lot.

Gripping my cock, I ran my hand up and down my hardness while grasping her panties in my other hand. I missed a woman's pussy. I missed tasting, eating, licking, and fucking one. It'd been too long just using my hand.

I wrapped her panties around my cock; the feeling caused me to groan. Closing my eyes and resting my head back against the headboard, images bombarded my mind.

Mena in nothing but those panties.

Mena opening my door to see what I was doing. Catching me with her panties, and then she'd say I didn't need them. She'd want to help me out.

Slowly, she'd strip her clothes from her body. I'd lick my lips from seeing her plump breasts on display. She'd crawl onto the bed at the end and look up at me hungrily. She'd want my cock in her mouth. My sunshine would beg for it. Still, I'd say no. I'd ask her to sit on her arse and open her legs to display her pretty pussy, and she'd do it, knowing how obsessed I was with her pussy.

Fuck, since I'd told her about my club name, each morning she'd come into the house with pink cheeks. I wished to Christ I had enough balls to see if she wanted me to show her how much I loved pussy, but I hadn't.

Soon, I'd change that.

Soon, I'd get a taste.

Hell, I was close to coming, so I slowed down my rhythm.

Didn't stop the images flooding my mind. Of Mena sitting on the end of her bed, facing me with her legs spread. I'd ask her to touch herself.

She'd smile shyly at first.

Her eyes would lower, but gently, she'd reach out a hand and glide it over her soft flesh. Right to the spot, I wanted her to go. Her back would arch at the first touch, and I'd wish it was my hand touching her. She'd moan as she slid two fingers inside herself. Then all my restraint would be out the window. I'd grab her ankles and pull her towards me. Then I'd wrap my hand around her waist and sit her on my lap where she'd lean back so I could dip my own fingers in, pull them out, and suck her wetness off them.

My sunshine would be panting, wanting more from

me and I'd give it to her. I'd bring her forward and line up my cock to her tight hole. Slowly, teasingly, she'd lower herself down on me. Her pussy would fit like a glove, like it was made for me.

"Fuck," I growled as my cum burst out of me, landing on my stomach. It kept coming as I ran my hand up and down, faster and faster.

I hadn't come that hard in a helluva long time. Christ, exhaustion took hold right after.

I slammed my hand over to my nightstand where I'd placed tissues there earlier that morning, knowing what I'd be doing that night.

I cleaned myself up and slid the panties back under my pillow before I rolled to my side and fell right to sleep.

SOMETHING DRAGGED me from my sleep. I was sitting before I knew it and my ears strained to work out what had woken me. That was when I heard a cry.

"Shit, Koda." Sleep disappearing, adrenaline pumped in my veins. My son never woke crying, so I knew something was wrong. Jumping out of bed, I ran from my room and straight to him.

Mena was standing there in, fuck me, a tee and panties.

"Is he okay?" I asked. My heart felt like it was in my throat.

She jumped, not hearing me arrive over Koda's crying. She spoke up to be heard over his wailing. "I was just about to get in the shower when I heard him. My guess is he's not feeling well." As if Koda wanted to prove her guess, he vomited all over the front of himself and Mena. Then started crying again. "Oh, sweet boy. It's okay. We'll get cleaned up." She turned to me, "Do you—" She gasped and closed her eyes. "Kalen." My name was a moan. Looking down, I realised in my panic, I'd run from my room naked.

"Shit. I heard him crying and just came running." My dick grew stiff; he wanted to show off for his sunshine.

"You sleep naked," she commented, peeked out her eyes, and closed them again tightly, and then her already blushing cheeks deepened and dipped down to her neck. She jiggled Koda gently in her arms and finally his cry settled to a whimper. Poor boy, being sick sucked, but first, they both needed to get clean before I could take care of him.

Chuckling, I stepped up to them and said, "Head for the bathroom, babe. Need to clean you both, and I'll be there to grab Koda from you once he's clean. I'll even put on some boxers." I steered them to the doorway. "Unless you don't want me to."

Another chuckle when she didn't answer straight

away, as if she was thinking about it. "No, um, boxers would be good."

I couldn't resist. As we hit the hall, I leaned in and kissed her shoulder. She stiffened until I tapped her arse and said, "Bathroom."

"Um, right." She nodded and started for the door. I walked off to my room, though I looked back just as she was going through the doorway to see her eyes on my arse. When I caught her, her eyes widened. I threw her a wink before she disappeared in the bathroom.

With black boxers on, I stepped into the bathroom to find Mena, still in her clothes, was already standing under the spray of water with Koda in her arms.

"Just called my boss. Told him I wasn't coming in today."

"You didn't have to do that. I can take care of him."

"I know you can, but I wanna be here for him." Her eyes warmed, and she nodded. "How's he doing?"

"Can you help me undress him? Then I'll wash him down, and we can get him dry. He'll need medicine to settle his stomach."

"Yeah, sounds like a plan." I got in the shower and stood just out of the spray. I didn't want to get wet and freeze my balls off while I took care of Koda, and Mena showered the puke off her. Reaching out, I grabbed Koda under the arms and held him out while Mena quickly got his clothes off and washed him down with his baby soap.

At least he seemed to like the shower. He wasn't crying, just in his own thoughts, watching. Kissing his temple, I told him, "You'll be okay, buddy." He tried to reach up to my face, but he was held out too far. Ah, fuck it. I brought him back to my chest, and his hand reached up for my beard, absently playing with it.

"He looks so tired. How did he sleep last night?"

"Good. Not a peep outta him."

She smiled sadly. "He'll need more sleep today, though. I doubt we'll be doing much."

"Sounds good to me. Lazy day it is until my boy is back to himself."

"He's ready to hop out."

"Thanks, you get cleaned up. I'll get him dry and dressed. Then we'll swap, and I'll have a shower."

"Okay."

Before hopping out of the shower, though, I leaned in and kissed her cheek. I heard her suck in her breath. When I pulled back, my eyes locked on hers. "Thanks, sunshine. Couldn't have done it without you."

Looking up through hooded eyes, she said, "Yes, you could have, but thank you."

After wrapping the towel around my boy, and just as I was out the bathroom door, I turned back to see her watching me and said, "Call out if you need a hand." With a wink, I walked out, but I didn't miss her mouth drop open, her eyes widen, or her cheeks heat.

Quickly dressing Koda, worry seeped into my mind. Fuck, I hoped he was going to be okay. Maybe I should call in a doctor just in case. The one good thing though was if it was just a stomach bug, I wouldn't have to use that snot sucker this time around.

CHAPTER NINETEEN

MENA

My heart went out to Koda. I hated seeing him sick. At least his dad stayed at home to help take care of him. Despite doing everything we could to get him feeling better, I wondered if we should call the house doctor in as a just in case. Kalen was a worrier, so if a doctor came, it would ease his mind.

The thought of Kalen, in all his naked glory, had been a welcome shock.

With his good-looking penis staring at me.

Even if all for a second, because I'd stupidly closed my eyes and missed my chance to take in his whole body.

Instead, I stored the bare glimpse to memory, so I could use it at night when I pictured him…

Then, he'd kissed my shoulder. I was sure I hadn't imagined it. It was a light peck, but still, I'd felt it down to my toes. In fact, they'd curled, and my vagina got over her anger at me. After the swat on the butt, I'd nearly died; my heart had beat so hard in my chest. Of course, I couldn't not look back when I knew he would be walking to his room, and I managed to see his sculpted bottom. His arms were covered in delicious tattoos, but his back, only one sat right in the middle. It was of a Hawk. Not that I looked longingly at him like I had his butt. When he'd caught me, I'd almost swallowed my tongue.

If I hadn't been so sore below and I could have taken longer in the shower, I would have touched myself, and I knew I would have come fast from everything that I'd seen, and he'd done.

By the time I was dressed and walking out of the bathroom, I found Kalen in the kitchen with a grumpy Koda in his high chair.

"I was thinking maybe we should ring a doctor?" I suggested.

Kalen grunted while he concentrated on measuring out Koda's medicine. When he turned, he said, "I was thinking the same thing. Can you do it while I give him this and see if he'll eat anything? If not, I'll get him to have some water."

Walking to Koda, I felt his forehead; heat pressed against my skin. Gently, I kissed him on the forehead, and he looked up at me and offered a quick smile. Then his attention went to his dad when Kalen stepped up.

"Are they good at taking this?"

"Usually kids love the taste of it," I reassured him and added, "At least you don't have to suck the snot out this time. Actually,"—I started for the living room where one of the phones were—"I'm surprised you didn't dry heave when Koda vomited."

"Not funny, woman."

Laughing, I went and made a call.

Koda spent the morning napping on and off on the couch covered in towels. We'd piled cushions on the floor in case we weren't quick enough to catch him. Still, we made sure one of us was sitting on the couch with him to try to catch the vomit. The doctor arrived late afternoon.

A brooding Kalen stood behind the couch with his arms crossed over his chest. He glared down at the doctor as he checked Koda all over while simultaneously glancing at me over and over. I was sitting on the couch with Koda in my lap because Koda started crying when the doctor got close. I was convinced Kalen chose not to sit with Koda in case he had to attack the doctor for some reason.

The doctor stood and smiled down at me. "Are you his aunt?"

"No, I'm—"

"What's that got to do with my kid? Just tell us what's going on."

The doctor blanched and stepped back. "Yes, it seems to be just a stomach bug. Nothing serious. All he needs is what you're already doing. Rest, a heap of fluids, and Panadol at the appropriate time. Don't worry if he doesn't eat. He may not want to at all even."

"Right." Kalen grunted.

I stood, placed Koda back to lie on the couch, and said, "Thank you for coming, Doctor. Mr Brooks will fix up the bill by the end of the day." I took his arm and led him to the door. A low rumble started behind me. Glancing over my shoulder, I saw Kalen's eyes zoned in on my hand on the doctor's arm. I quickly removed it and opened the door. The doctor stepped out. He turned as if to say something, but I blurted out, "Have a great afternoon and thanks again," before shutting the door after him.

Spinning around, I glared and said, "Why would you act like that when he was here to help Koda?"

He rolled his eyes, moved around the couch, and sat with his son. "The good old doctor was too busy staring at your tits and legs than examining Koda."

My eyes widened. "He was not. And you shouldn't swear so much in front of Koda."

"He was. And Koda will learn what is wrong and right."

Throwing my hands up in the air, I asked, "Do you want to get another doctor to visit for a second opinion?"

"No."

"So you trust what he said."

He shrugged. "He is a doctor, despite all the perving he did. Next time, you don't touch him."

Exasperated, I snapped, "I was just leading him to the door."

"Don't touch him," he shot back roughly.

"Why not?" I demanded.

"Because I don't like seeing it."

Silence pierced the air until I whispered, "Oh." Shuffling a foot, I said, "Um, I'm going to start dinner and see if anything will coax Koda into eating. I'll also fill up his drink bottle and do some cleaning."

Kalen looked from his son to me with a smirk on his lips. "Yeah, you do that, sunshine."

Yes, I was running from the heart-palpitations situation, but I needed to sort out my mind. Kalen, it seemed, was acting interested in me. More than his housekeeper and more than Koda's nanny. I wasn't sure how to take it, but I knew my body loved the idea of Kalen showing interest; at least, that was what I thought he was doing. I didn't have much experience in men. Mark was my only lover, and we'd grown up together. Everything about this was different. Fresh, exciting, and new.

Still, I was concerned I was convenient for him.

He missed his wife.

But he also said he missed her for Koda's sake.

I knew Koda was more important to Kalen than going out and finding a woman to spend the night with, or an hour just to get his jollies off. So I was back to my first thought. I was convenient.

However, was my mind supplying that thought so I could keep him at arm's length still?

Could be a possibility.

All right, it was more than likely, but of course, I was scared about Kalen showing interest, even when it thrilled me at the same time. Exasperated with myself and my internal battle, I attempted to shrug thoughts of Kalen away and concentrated on preparing food.

For dinner, I made a vegetable soup with warm, homemade bread rolls. Even if Koda didn't eat the vegetables, but had the stock instead, he would be getting some nutrition. I walked into the living room with two bowls on a tray. "Dinner."

"Smells fuckin' awesome, sunshine." Kalen sat up and helped a very tired Koda sit also.

He went to take Koda's bowl, but I said, "No, you eat yours. I'll sit on the floor and feed Koda. He won't be in the mood to do anything himself."

"Thanks, babe."

Blushing, I said, "Not a problem." After Kalen had taken his, I placed the tray on the coffee table, sat on the floor, and spooned some to Koda. He was happily taking it, and after he refused about the tenth spoonful, I offered him a small buttered roll. He took it, but I knew he wouldn't be eating much.

Glancing out the corner of my eyes, I saw Kalen watching us both with a smile on his lips. Though, seeing it caused the question I'd thought of while I'd been making dinner to pop back into my mind. I was worried I would soon be losing the chance to look upon his smile. "Kalen?"

"Yeah, sunshine?"

"I was, um, if you don't mind my asking. I was wondering, you've said you'll eventually move back to Caroline Springs."

Tipping his bowl, he drank the last of his soup before placing the bowl on the coffee table and sitting back, his arms stretching along the back of the couch and armrest.

"Yeah, Mena. My home is back there. Fuck, I've been missing it for a while now. Love being around my brothers, working in the garage, and living in the place I have."

"You already have a place?"

He smiled. "Sure do. Live right next door to Dodge and Low. Three-bedroom brick home. Much like this really, and since I've been here a while now and gotten to love it, I'll keep this place and have it as a family retreat. Any time one of my brothers or even me wants to get away, we'll have this place."

My eyes widened. "You own this place also?"

"Fuck yeah. Had mum search for the right place before Koda was released from hospital. She knew what I'd like and picked the perfect spot. I got some money behind me, sunshine. Not only from what Dad had left me in his will, but I got my share in some of Talon's strip clubs over Victoria." He shrugged, looking around the room. "Now that I've lived here for a while, I can't find it in me to get rid of it. Still, can't find it in me to desert my brothers forever. I need to get back there."

"How come you moved in the first place?"

He shrugged and looked to Koda, so I did also. He was back to lying down, his eyes fluttering open and closed. "Stress. I'd just lost Simone and found out I was a father. My head was full of shit. The pain was too much. I needed an out and moving to somewhere new was the answer at the time."

"I can understand that." And I could. I'd moved to Halls Gap for a new start. Losing so much in life could push you to do wild, strange things. At least a change of scenery was all Kalen and I did.

"Sunshine."

Looking up, I said, "Hmm?"

"When I go back, you got anything to hold you here, or would you come and continue doing what you do?"

Oh, wow.

Tingles spread through my body. My heart told me to get up and jump for joy like it already was in my chest, but I didn't. Instead, I bit my bottom lip. My body stiffened, and I thought over and over, *Don't cry, don't cry.*

He wanted me to go with him.

He wasn't prepared to leave me behind.

Though, did it also mean it was all for Koda? Kalen wanted me with him *just* for Koda?

Which in a way, I didn't mind if I was. I knew I was good at my job because I loved my time with Koda. I loved cooking and cleaning.

But, a small part of me hoped *he* was asking because *he* didn't want to see me gone. *He* hated the thought of never seeing me again.

"I—" Clearing my throat, I started again. "I have nothing holding me here, but I'll have to find somewhere to live." With the money I was saving, it could go towards a small bedroom, sharing with other people.

"We'll see how things go. I'm not ready anytime soon. Besides, Mum would kick my arse if I up and left when she was away."

A giggle fell from my lips. "She would." And now I found myself thinking about how much I would miss her when we moved. I already missed her when she was off with her friends travelling, using the money she got when her husband passed. When I moved, I'd miss her more.

"We'd come see her," Kalen said as if he read my mind. "Like I said, I'd keep this place, and we'd come up any time we wanted."

His words embedded in my chest. *Us. We.* Every time he talked about moving, he included me in it, and it sounded like more than just as his worker. At least it did to me.

CHAPTER TWENTY

ONE WEEK LATER

DIVE

Even though I'd gone back to work the day after Koda got sick, I wanted to stay home. It wasn't because of my boy. No, he was back to himself since it was a twenty-four-hour bug. It was because of Philomena McAdams.

I wanted her time, her company, her heart, her mind, and in between her legs.

She seemed to want me as well. Her eyes followed me

everywhere, or she'd seek me out, even if Koda was in bed, to spend time with me. We'd talk about anything and everything. She'd smile shyly, she'd blush, and maybe it was accidently, but she'd brush against me, and my dick would harden.

Wrong.

My dick was hard all the goddamn time.

My patience was wearing thin.

I wanted her to be the one to make a move, but I could see she wouldn't. She'd be worried. Worried, she'd lose her job, lose us, if things failed between us.

I wouldn't let it fail.

She was it.

The time we'd had together, getting to know each other, told me she was it. We were meant to be. I was meant to move, meant to meet her and have sunshine in my life.

Today, I was going to show her how my life worked; see if anything she saw she hated or if it scared her. If her cute-as-fuck chin jutted out and up, showing nothing fazed her, then she was the right one for me. It would mean somehow, somewhere, someone was looking down upon me and sent me to the right area to find her.

Stalking out of my bedroom, I found Mena in the kitchen doing the morning dishes. Even though we had a dishwasher, she still liked to wash them by hand. Leaning against the doorframe, I crossed my arms over my chest and waited for her to know I was watching. Didn't take long, though. That was because my son in his high chair scribbling with crayons yelled, "Dada."

Mena jumped and spun to face me in the doorway. Her wide eyes narrowed. "What are you doing?"

"Decided to go for a drive."

"Okay, um, you know I'll take care of Koda." She shrugged and rolled her eyes like I was being silly.

"Also decided you're coming." I smirked when she stiffened. "Gonna go see my brothers in Caroline Springs. Wanna make it back by tonight, so get shit organised to leave ASAP, babe."

"But, um,"—she looked around the kitchen—"I have things that need to be done."

"Like what? It's the weekend, sunshine. You don't usually do anything on the weekend." She was so full of shit. She was scared because she knew I'd be taking her where the most important people in my life were.

"Well, maybe I need to, um… I promised Judy I would tidy her house before she got home on Monday."

My smile was a teasing one. "Bullshit. Babe, you're coming."

"No."

"Mena," I growled the word and glared.

Her hands went to her hips while her chin jutted out and up in her defiant stand. "I have things to do, Kalen."

"Mena, you can either get in the car on your own, or I'll carry you there." I raised a brow at her.

"You wouldn't."

"You know me by now, woman. I'll do it, and I'll enjoy doing it because I'll get to feel your body over my shoulder while I have the chance to cop a feel of your arse at the same time." Crimson flared across her cheeks, and her eyes widened. She proceeded to open and close her mouth like a dying fish. "Why don't you grab your purse and Koda's bag in the living room? I'll meet you out in the car."

"Um." She licked her lips. "Okay?" It came out as a question, but she started to move even before she'd finished saying it. A few words were grumbled as she passed while I chuckled.

By the time I got Koda out to the car, she was waiting in the front seat with a scowl upon her sweet face. I strapped Koda in, who was happy to get in the car; he loved going for a drive. He picked up his car toys and started playing and talking to himself. When I got in, my eyes went right to her legs.

Fuck.

She was wearing those damn denim shorts. I should've told her to change because I knew my brothers would be eye-fucking her legs the whole day. I just hoped to Christ I didn't have to hurt any of them.

As we headed down the drive, I explained, "We're gonna go to where I used to work. It's also a part of the compound my brothers hang out in. Want everyone to meet Koda." And Mena… I wanted to show them all what had brought me outta my darkness. Wanted everyone to see my sunshine.

"Um, okay. Not sure why I had to come, but okay." Her hands restlessly fiddled together on her lap.

"Don't you wanna see where you'll be moving to? We'll also go to my house. Low's set up Koda's room, but she did that a while ago, so things will probably need to be updated. You can work out what we'll need."

"Low mentioned there was a room at Nary's apartment I could probably rent—"

"No," I barked.

"Sorry?"

Gripping the steering wheel, I fought my anger at Low for even mentioning Simone's old room. What in the fuck had she been thinking?

"Kalen?"

I ran a hand through my hair, let out a heavy breath, and said, "That was Simone's old room." She gasped. There was no way in hell I'd want to see Mena in my old woman's place. Too many memories. Too much to drag up from the past. Not that I was there much. Simone used to always come to me, but fuck, my last memories were when she went into labour, and then not long after, I'd lost her.

"I don't know why Low would—"

"Doesn't matter," I muttered harshly. "Just drop it." And those were the last words I'd said before we pulled into the compound car park.

Shit, I was being a dick again, but bringing up Simone had put a downer on my mood. I didn't even fucking get it. Maybe guilt was a part of it because the way I was feeling about Mena. Hell, I had to let that guilt go. I had to, or else I'd never get on with my life, and I wanted to. I wanted to thrive in the feeling Mena put in my heart. Crap, I sounded like a sappy dickwad.

Turning to Mena in the car, she was just about to get out, her hand on the door handle, but I reached over and placed my hand on hers.

"Sorry. Fuck, Mena. I close up and get shitty every time I talk about Simone, and I shouldn't. I was a dick snapping at you. It won't happen again. I need to make sure Koda remembers his mum like she wanted him to," I explained.

Her eyes focused on outside. Some brothers walked by or around the car. Still, they kept to themselves, knowing something was going on in the car. "You should start already with Koda. Show him photos of her, talk about her. Call her his mum. He's a gorgeous little boy, and she was a huge part of making him. He deserves to know who his mum is and what he meant to her and how much you both love her." She nodded to herself.

"Loved," I corrected.

Her eyes met mine, our faces close because I still held my hand over hers. "Sorry?" she whispered.

"Loved, Mena. How much I *loved* her. I'll always miss her, like you will Mark, and she still holds a part of my heart because of Koda and what we *had*, but that's it."

Her chest heaved up and down. Her eyes widened a fraction, and since I was still close, my eyes drifted down to her mouth, and I watched as her tongue peeked out and wet her lips.

We both jumped when something hit the bonnet. I pulled back and glared out the front window, only to smile seconds later when my eyes spotted Jason, Blue's younger brother.

"Hey, Dive." He grinned, took a hand up, and waved at us through the window.

A chuckle left my mouth. I opened my door and got out. Walking right to him, he stood tall and opened his arms for me. With a quick hug and a pat on the back, he pulled back and asked, "Did I interrupt something? It looked too intense in the car. Then again, it looked like you were about to kiss her. If I stuffed up, I could go, and you can get back in the car and kiss her. She's real pretty. Like really pretty. Not as hot as my woman, but still nice." He leaned in and whispered, "Could be as good as Clary, and that's saying something." He shoved my arm and laughed. "Do you want to get back in the car and—" A door slammed. We looked at the car to see Mena already out and with Koda in her arms. "Crap, too late now."

Jason was like a puppy, overexcited and go, go, go all the time. He was a great kid. Though, I couldn't say kid really; he was nearly twenty. He'd been to Ballarat to do his prospecting for his position in Hawks under the watchful eye of his brother. He'd only recently moved back. It was more for his protection than anything, so everyone knew not to fuck with him. He was also still in uni doing some computer course. Not that he really needed to be. He was fucking smarter than most. He got with his woman on his eighteenth birthday. We'd all come to celebrate it with him, and she'd stuck to him like glue since. She was a sweet, shy girl. We were all happy for him.

Placing my arm around his shoulder, I turned us to Mena and said, "Jason, this is Koda, my son, and the woman holding him is Mena, ah…" Shit, should I say, *"my woman?"* Didn't think that one through at all.

"Hi, Jason." Mena smiled. I felt Jason stiffen. "I'm Koda's nanny."

He leaned into me and said, what he thought was a whisper, "When she smiles, better than Clary."

My own smile was huge and it widened to a cocky grin when I saw Mena blush. Pretending to whisper, I informed him, "Couldn't agree more." Standing tall, I reached out for Koda, who came into my arms. Once he was on my hip, I tagged Mena around the shoulder with my free arm. "Babe, Jason is Blue's brother, a Hawks brother, and also a computer genius."

"He forgot more good-looking than most." Jason grinned. "But, I'm also taken. Sorry, Mena."

My woman giggled. "That's okay, Jason. I'm just glad to meet you."

"Same. Though, I have to get going. I promised my beauty I'd take her for a ride, and then Mum wants to do some family dinner thing tonight." He rolled his eyes, stepped forward, and grabbed Mena from my arms into a hug. "Take care of Dive."

When he pulled back, she offered him a wink, her cheeks lightening up once again.

"Later, brother." His fist came out. I hit it with my own and gave him a chin lift before he took off on a jog towards his own Harley. Blue and his mum worried about him and his bike every fucking day. Still, he wanted one, and he got one because he said he wasn't a real brother until he had one. That kid was kickarse.

Looking back to Mena, I asked, "You ready?"

"Um, if all your friends are like Jason, then yes."

Chuckling, I took her hand in mine and led her towards the front office where I knew Low would be working. "You'll see."

Opening the door, Low squealed, "Give me some lovin', handsome." I knew she was talking to my son. Still, I held out my arms and smirked. Low rolled her eyes and said, "Wasn't talking to you." She took Koda out of my arms and held him close, showering him with kisses all over his face. He giggled the whole time, loving the attention.

The office door opened and in stalked Dodge with a smile. "Brother." With a slap to my back, he then turned to Mena, who squeaked in surprise when he brought her into his arms for a hug. "Good to see ya, Mena."

"Y-you too." She smiled shyly.

Dodge looked to me and said, "Why don't you go show Mena around? We'll watch Koda."

Smirking, I noted, "Sounds like a plan." Which was what had been my intention. I'd rang Dodge early that morning, telling him about my decision with Mena, how she was moving with us when the time came. How I wanted her in my house, in my life more than what she was. I wanted her as my woman. But first, I wanted to see how she handled my brothers, coped around the compound, especially when she discovered what went on when my brothers were tying one on. It was the weekend, so I knew many would be enjoying their downtime.

"I can stay here with Koda if you want to go see your friends."

"Babe." I chuckled. "They're my brothers, and you're

coming with me." Taking her hand, I walked her out the office and into the mechanical area. Though, I didn't miss the big eyes she gave Low or the wink Low offered back.

Fuck, I hoped Mena could handle everything she was about to see.

CHAPTER TWENTY-ONE

MENA

Vomit was slowly crawling up my throat, giving me heartburn. Or was my heart just burning because my nerves were all over the place? Why did he want to show me around? Why was it important for me to meet his frie—brothers?

I was already on my last bit of strength. Especially after I heard Jason saying it looked like Kalen was about to kiss me, and then *he* didn't deny it either. At the time, I had felt like he was going to touch his lips to mine. I was grateful he didn't because then Koda would have been witness to me losing my mind and devouring his father.

While we walked through the garage, all men said a

hello to Kalen, but calling him Dive, and they eyed first our joined hands and then the length of me. Suddenly, I felt like I was under a microscope.

We came to a door at the side of the garage. I could already hear the music behind it, but before he opened it, he turned to me and said, "Remember, sunshine, we're bikers here. We like to party, live hard, and fuck just as hard." I blushed, and he smirked. "We're loud and can be full on, but never be scared. You'll always be protected. Not just by me, but all my brothers will have your back. It's what Hawks and the brotherhood is about."

Studying his face, I saw by his pinched brow that he was nervous about taking me in there. I wanted to reassure him I'd be okay. Anything he showed me, I could handle, but I'd heard stories about bikers. They were rough and scary, so I wasn't sure I could reassure him at that point. Still, I found myself offering a calming smile and saying, "Don't worry. If I can handle your moods, I can handle some bikers."

He threw his head back and laughed loudly. When it turned into a chuckle, he shook his head and said, "We'll see." Then he opened the door.

As soon as we stepped into the large room, cheers rang out. They'd spotted Kalen right away and started for him. He let go of my hand as the first arrived and took him into a manly hug. My eyes gazed around; there were at least twenty men around the room, which held a pool table, couches, a bar, tables, and chairs. And there were about ten women, all partially dressed, and there I thought I would feel bare in my jean shorts. I watched the women, after the men had greeted Kalen, wind themselves back around their flavour for the day.

I'd heard of them before. I'd just never knew they really existed. They were club bunnies. They lived to serve the bikers in any sexual way the men wanted.

My stomach pivoted. My hands started to sweat. I wasn't sure how I felt about them being there. Had Kalen used them?

My eyes had already judged them as tarts, where I felt like I shouldn't have. I didn't know their reason for what they did. Anything in their life could have brought them to where they were. Who was I to judge women for what they did, and who was I to judge the men for enjoying something that was given to them freely?

If everyone was happy in their own situation, and no one was being harmed, it was none of my business what went on.

Well, as long as Kalen wasn't using the women. If he was, it would be a different story. If he wanted someone to warm his bed, then I would be that one. I wouldn't let a woman who'd pleased so many claw their way into Kalen and Koda's life.

"Mena?"

Looking to Kalen, I realised I was so busy with my

own thoughts that it hadn't been the first time he'd called. Concern marred his face. His brows raised in question, asking if I was okay.

I sent a warm smile to Kalen, letting him know I was okay. Later, I would ask Kalen about his part with the house women, even knowing I would blush the whole way through it.

His shoulders seemed to sag in relief. He gestured with his hand to come to his side, but before I could make a step, my name was bellowed, and then I was lifted off the floor and into some strong manly arms.

"Mena, babe. How you doin'? So good to see you here." I was set on my feet, and I nearly teetered back if it wasn't for Knife placing his hands on my shoulders as he smiled down at me. "What you doin'? Come all this way to see me 'cause you missed me? Damn, woman, you look good enough to eat."

The room went quiet except for the music still drumming into the room. Tension filled the room; it was like a pulse touching my skin.

"Um," I started.

"Knife. I'd step back if I were you," a gruff voice said, only it held humour as well. Glancing to my side, it had come from Dallas. I was about to say hello when I felt warmth at my back. My head went back and up to see Kalen standing there with a snarl on his face.

"You wanna let her go, or I'd be willing to help out."

"Come on, brother." Knife smiled. "She's just your kid's nanny." Someone whistled low. Others swore, and some chuckled.

"She's mine." Hardness formed his words.

My body stiffened. *What does that mean?*

"You're not messin', right?" Knife smirked.

"Tell me, what would Pick or Billy do to you if you touched Josie?"

"Beat me senseless."

What?

"Take that as your only warning. If you touch Mena again, I'll do the same."

Knife stepped back one and smiled. "You claimin'?"

"Yes," he growled.

Huh?

Knife laughed then. "'Bout fuckin' time."

The room filled with booming noise. I wanted to cover my ears, but I couldn't because next I was being taken by the hand and dragged towards a hall. Kalen kept going, down a long hall, and still the shouting, cheers, and clapping behind us didn't die down until we were in a room with the door shut.

Kalen leaned against the door and tugged me close. I had to let go of his hand and place them on his chest, so I didn't fall from his fast movement.

Looking up, I saw his eyes were hard, but something

else shone in his steel eyes. "What was that about?" I whispered.

"Me stating something." His voice was low and gravely.

My eyes darted to the side and then back to him. "What?" I whispered again.

"Kiss me and I'll tell you," he demanded.

My stomach dipped and quivered. My clit was along for the ride as well. "What?" I repeated, releasing an exhale.

He leaned in, his eyes eating me up, searching my face before stopping on my wide eyes. "Hated seein' his hands on you. It was the last straw, Mena. You. Are. Mine." His lips crashed down on mine. I froze for a second until he leaned further in with his hands behind my thighs and picked me up. I wrapped my arms around his shoulders, my legs around his waist, and tilting my head, I deepened the kiss. It felt desperate. We couldn't get enough of each other's taste, feel, heat. It had been a build-up of lust, tension, and need for so long. But it was over. I *had* him. Against me, in my arms. His lips were finally on my mouth, my tongue sliding with his in such a wicked way.

It was more than I imagined, and I'd done a lot of imagining.

He pulled back, his forehead against mine. "Fuck." He growled the word before his mouth took mine once again.

We were moving. He walked until my back hit a soft mattress. He'd kept my attention since we'd entered, so I hadn't realised we were in a bedroom. Still, I didn't care where we were as long as he stayed in my arms.

My hands clawed at his tee. I wanted so much more from him but was too nervous still to ask for it.

I tipped back my head when he trailed his lips down my neck. I gasped for breath as he bit, licked, and sucked. "Let me touch. Fuck, sunshine, just a small touch until we get home. Need something to tide me over," he mumbled against my skin. I didn't understand what he was asking for, but at that moment, I was ready to give him anything he asked for. So I nodded and then moaned, "Yes," when he bit hard on my collarbone.

His hand slid from my hair, down my shoulder, my arm, and then it went to my waist all while I lost myself in his scent, his touch, and body against me, surrounding me. My chest heaved in excitement when I felt his fingers at the button of my shorts. He undid it and lowered the zipper.

Maybe I should have stopped him. Maybe I should have thought about his brothers and the women in the other room. However, Kalen consumed my mind. His fingers danced slowly along the top of my panties, and his mouth glided back up my neck to kiss me like I was the last woman on earth.

When his fingers dipped in and touched my clit, I

moaned against his mouth. His hips thrust into my side, and I felt, *felt* how turned on he was from just touching me. His fingers slid down further and circled around my entrance, only to drag my wetness back up to my clit.

"Fina-fuckin'-lly, I get to touch your sweet, bare pussy," he groaned. My legs spread further, giving him better access. My hand gripped his tee tightly.

"Kalen." I breathed an annoyed mew against his lips when his fingers suddenly stopped and rested against my mound.

"What do you need, sunshine?"

"Please," I begged, my eyes searching his heated and amused ones.

"Tell me what you want, Mena."

Glaring, I ordered, "Fucking touch me."

The annoying man chuckled, kissed my lips, and said, "My woman has a dirty mouth when she's horny."

My woman.

He'd said my woman.

I was his.

He was claiming me.

That was what all that meant in the other room.

Digging my heels into the bed, I thrust my hips up and snapped, "Touch me, Kalen. Make me come if I'm your woman."

His eyes darkened. A snarl rumbled up out of his chest. "Gladly." Two fingers swept straight into me. I moaned loudly, my hips swivelled up and down, riding his fingers. "Yeah, sunshine. Fuck yourself on me." I was so wet, so close. I was lost in all what Kalen was doing to me.

His mouth trailed down again as I rode his fingers in and out of me. It wasn't until I felt his teeth take my nipple into his mouth over my tee did I yell, "Fuck, yes." Then he bit down and thrust his fingers hard into me. When his thumb touched my clit, my orgasm came over me quickly. I grabbed his wrist and helped his hand enter in and out of me while my walls convulsed around his fingers.

As soon as I came down, my whole body sagged into the mattress. My legs flattened to the bed and with tired eyes, I looked up at Kalen and smiled. His fingers slid out of me. My body jolted at the loss, and then he brought his fingers to his mouth and licked my juices off them.

"Christ," he hissed. "Can't wait to eat you out, Mena. You gonna open up and give me your cunt to devour?"

Oh. My. God.

My clit pulsated. If he kept talking like that, I would probably come again.

He smiled and said roughly, "Yeah, my woman likes the thought of her man's mouth on her wet pussy."

The orgasm fog cleared, and I asked in a quiet voice, "So, this means we're, um, together?"

He threw his head back and roared with laughter.

Then he leaned his forehead into my shoulder while he chuckled some more.

Pulling back, he said with a smile. "Yeah, sunshine. We're together."

Forgetting my annoyance at him laughing at me, I grinned widely and whispered, "Awesome."

His hand came to my cheek, and he whispered back, after a small kiss on my lips, "Yeah, awesome." His next move was to sit up a bit, do up my shorts, and then he said words no woman would want to hear after coming so hard. "Still, we have to talk."

DIVE

While she was in a happy state, I thought it best to share some shit with her. Even if all I wanted to do was bury my aching cock inside her sweet tasting tight hole, I held back. She had to know all of me before choosing to take it all on.

"Um," which was her standard reply while she got what she wanted to say in her head in order. "Okay," she said hesitantly, sitting up next to me.

Smiling, I reassured her, "Nothin' too bad. At least I think, but I wanna tell you everything before you jump on board with us."

"Hit me." She nodded, all ready to jump right in.

"Fuck, you're gorgeous." I threaded my fingers tight in her hair and planted my lips on hers. My tongue demanded entrance, and she gave it to me right away. Then, I broke apart and stood. "Shit," I hissed. "I can't keep kissing you or we won't get outta this room. And if things go right after we talk, I wanna get Koda and get the fuck home to put him to bed. 'Cause all I can think of right now is you spread out on my bed naked."

Jesus. She rubbed her thighs together. She loved that plan.

"Right." I stared down at her with my hands on my hips. "Stop looking so fuckable, dammit."

She giggled. My cock jerked behind my jeans. "I'll get right on that." She smiled.

"Smart-arse." I laughed. "All right. Has Low said anything to you about what happened to her?"

MENA

I knew what he was talking about. Low's family had been terrible. All of them users in one way. I was shocked when she'd told me her cousin tried to sell her. Again, I'd heard some things like that happening in the world. I never imagined it would be in Australia.

"Yes, some of it."

"The thing is, the man who was meant to buy her is still causing shit. He's got a problem with Hawks, and by Hawks, it's with whoever is a member. We're being careful. We're on a hunt for the fucktard, and he will pay for the shit he's doing and by pay, I mean in blood." My eyes widened. He got to his knees in front of me and took my hands in his. "Sunshine, I need you to understand when getting into it with me, I've done shit the cops would lock me up for, but all of it was for a reason. All of it was deserved because they were scum and had fucked with Hawks. We don't go to the cops with our troubles. We deal with issues ourselves." He stopped and studied me.

What I was hearing, I got. How could I not? Kalen had done more for me in the time I'd known him than anyone. Not only him, but his brothers came and helped without a question. What Kalen had was a family, and they had each other's back no matter the cost. They fought and made sure nothing could harm anyone in their family.

Family came first.

Before anything else.

I could understand that.

"Mena, sunshine. It means more shit could still come our way. But I want you to know I'll protect you and Koda with everything I have. Nothing will harm you if I have anything to do with it. And that's the thing with

Hawks. You not only have my protection, but you also have my brothers' as well. That dick will not lay a finger on either of you. Do you trust that?"

Shaking my hands out of his, I reached up and cupped his face. His beard tickled my fingers, but I liked it, and I was looking forward to feeling it between my legs. "You have a big heart, Kalen Brooks. I trust anything you say. Well, as long as you aren't in a mood."

He smiled. "If I get in a mood and say shit to you, tell me to fuck off." A blush hit my cheeks. He laughed. "I forgot you only get a dirty mouth when you're horny." My hands slid to his chest and my forehead hit his shoulder so I could hide. His hand held the back of my neck. "Seriously, Mena. Don't take my shit."

"I won't," I whispered. He needed a strong woman in a relationship, and I would be one. I would stand up to him if it were something important to me. "As long as you know what you're asking for. I can be a tyrant when I want to be."

He snorted. "I'll believe it when I see it."

Leaning back, I asked, "Speaking of not taking your, um, doo-doo, not that it's really about that, but... whose room is this and will your brothers know what we just did? Also, from this day forward, I would like to try and keep our frolicking between just us."

Oh, God. I said frolicking.

Closing my eyes, I waited for it, and it didn't take long. Kalen's booming laughter filled the room. Only, my eyes flashed open in the next second because I didn't expect my whole body to be lifted and planted on Kalen's lap.

He cradled my head into the crook of his shoulder while his laughter wained. "Not sure what I did, but I'd fuckin' do it again and again if it was my luck that brought you into my life." My body stiffened while my heart sighed a big happy sigh on the inside. He felt lucky I'd come into his life. How was that possible when I was the lucky one? His hand slipped down from the back of my head to my lower back. There he circled his hand around and said, "Regret a lot of things. A top one would be the way I treated you when you first came into my life. I was a goddamn prick, sunshine. Sorry."

Leaning back to meet his eyes, I told him, "Honestly, I'm glad you weren't nice because if you were as you are now, I probably would have left. You would have made me flustered too much."

His smile was bright. "For the first time, I'll thank fuck for my arsehollery." He kissed me once and quickly before he added, "Back to your questions. This is my room in the compound. No one else uses it, and well, shit, yeah, they probably know something went down between us. Especially when you walk out there with those eyes, which are telling me you were well pleased." I scoffed and hit him in the chest. He grabbed my hand chuckling. "But you need to learn not to give a fuck about what other people think." He watched his hand as he slid it to the side of my neck, and then with his thumb, he reached around and ran it along my bottom lip. "No one should matter but you, me, and Koda. Love my brothers, sunshine, but it's us three who come first. So fuck 'em. Hold your head up high and walk out there with no care in the world. They may give us shit, but don't let it get to you. Seeing you come hard and sweet like that, with your filthy mouth and all. It was bloody worth any shit we get. It was something special. It was our special. And nothin' or no one can tarnish it by stupid words in jest."

My nerves were rattled, but he was right. What mattered, what counted more than anything was the three of us. Who cared what they thought? Who cared they knew we were getting active in the bedroom? I didn't. I couldn't, not when it meant so much to me. Not when it had to do with Kalen claiming me as his woman and dang it, I was claiming him as my man.

"No matter what, all I care about is having you and Koda around me. It's the two of you who make me happy. It's the two of you who have brought me something worth living for." Biting my bottom lip, I watched his eyes warm and lower at my words. "It's not just the orgasm talking." Humour lit his eyes, and his mouth twitched. Still, I went on, "I've been feeling special, lucky, for a while now, but I was scared to do or say anything. I'm scared of losing either of you because you both mean so much to me."

"I can't promise things will be all rainbows and shit between us, but I can promise you ain't losing me or Koda. We're in this and even when we argue, know that I won't walk out the door leaving you thinking we're over."

"Even if you tried, now I know you want to give us a go, I'd drag you back inside and lock you up until you saw reason."

"Sounds perfect to me."

"So glad I came today." I smiled.

"In more ways than one." Kalen chuckled.

Rolling my eyes, I laughed. "I suppose you could say that."

"If I'd known bringing you home would have given me the chance to have my hand in your pants, I would have done it a long time ago. A fuckin' long time ago."

"If I would have known jealousy would have—"

"Don't even say it," he said with a growl.

Laughing, I patted his chest and said, "Don't worry, I'm usually too shy around people, but you need to look out. My shyness is fading with you."

"Glad for it." He grinned. "Though, I'm sure I can get your cheeks to heat anytime I want."

Biting my bottom lip, I shook my head and then said, "I doubt that."

"Really?" he smirked.

"Yes." I nodded, knowing full well he could, but I wanted to see what he came up with to get me all embarrassed.

"Babe, are you missing a certain pair of panties?" My eyes widened. His smirk was cocky. "I'll give them to you tonight. For a week or so, I've been using them to wank over because the thought of your pussy is a temptation I couldn't resist. I needed something that was pressed close against it. Fuck, just thinkin' about it gets me hard. So hard, I'm thinking of layin' you back on the bed and slamming my cock into you. I know you'd like it. My woman with a dirty mouth would like a bit of dirty play."

Yes, my cheeks reddened. Only it wasn't really from embarrassment; it was because lust, red-hot and needy, pooled low in my belly, riding me hard and tempting me to take him up on his offer.

He ran the back of his fingers over my cheek. "Told you I could. Fuckin' love the fact, it's from you being turned on. Let's get back to Koda so we can get the fuck outta here soon?"

"Y-yes." I was more than ready. Standing from Kalen's lap, he took my hand, kissed me deep and hard and then stalked to the door, down the hall and out into the large room where a party was still happening. More cheers sounded. There were also slaps on the back for Kalen, and if some were brave, they even risked hugging me. But it was Dallas who whispered, "Good to have our smiling brother back. Thank you."

Tears threatened, but I held them back and nodded into his shoulder. It was then Kalen brought me close and placed his arm around my shoulders. He walked us the rest of the way to the office like that.

As soon as Kalen opened the office door, we stopped.

"He's just started," Low whispered as she came to our side. Dodge followed and tagged his woman with a hand to the back of the neck, bringing her to his front while we all stood back and watched Koda.

He was standing. With his hands on the office chair, he moved his feet up and down. He knew what he wanted to do. As if sensing his audience, he looked over and smiled. "Dada, Nena," he cried. My hand flew to cover my mouth. Kalen's arm around my shoulders tightened, and we watched in awe as Koda took his first steps towards us, only to fall to his bottom after three.

The room erupted in claps. I rushed to him and picked him up, twirling him, kissing him, and telling him what an amazing boy he was.

Kalen met my gaze with warm eyes and a soft smile on his lips. Then he spent the next hour talking with Dodge while Low and I got Koda to walk as much as he wanted to, before he cracked it from having enough.

Because we knew there was no rush for us. We had a lot of time on our hands, and we wanted to cherish every one of Koda's steps in life.

DIVE

Proud to see my son's first steps. Ecstatic my woman was with me when it happened, but now I was just horny as fuck. What didn't help was the whole drive home, while Mena talked and praised Koda, her hand rubbed my thigh unconsciously.

As we came into Halls Gap, I laid my hand over hers and asked, "What did Dodge say to you as we were leaving?" While Low was trying to keep my attention, my brother had pulled my woman aside and said something to her. Mena had smiled and nodded before she had quickly hugged my brother.

"Um," she started, looking from Koda in the back to

me. Out the corner of my eyes, I saw her nod to herself. "He said for a long time he was worried about you. But he knows he doesn't have to now."

Shit. My brother. Always had my back. Always worried. Fuck, I was the same with him. With all my brothers.

Picking up her hand, I kissed the back of it and said, "He's right. He's got nothing to worry about now. I'm happy."

"I'm glad I can bring that for you."

"So am I, sunshine." I smiled over at her. "We never made it to our house. We'll have to go back another weekend to get shit sorted."

"I'm all for it, and maybe Low and Dodge could mind Koda for a while." She winked. Fuck yeah, I liked the sound of that. And even though the house brought memories of Simone, it was time to start with new memories that would be just as good, if not better. But first, I was getting a new bed for me to share with my woman.

Like I'd said, Simone would always hold a part of my heart, but it was time to start living again.

Living with the woman who'd stolen the rest of my heart along with my boy.

When we arrived home, it was already late. We'd eaten takeaway on the way, so all we had to do was get Koda washed and into bed, which didn't take long. He'd worn himself out with all the walking he'd done. By the time I laid him in his crib, he was already half asleep.

Walking back out into the living room, I found Mena sitting on the couch. Her hand fidgeted with the hem of her shorts. She was nervous, and I couldn't help but smile.

"Mena." I aimed for a gentle tone, but it came out gruff. When her head snapped up, and her eyes met mine, I ordered, "Come here." She got up and took the steps needed to stop in front of me. My hands went to her waist, and I forced her close so our bodies touched. "Not sure why you're nervous, sunshine. I'm a sure thing tonight."

Humour spread through her eyes before she threw her head back and burst out laughing. Her laughter only stopped when I leaned in and licked the length of her neck. I felt my tee pull as her hands gripped it tightly. Placing a kiss on her shoulder, I stepped back to find her face flushed. I took her hand in mine and led her down the hallway to my room. A thrill ran over me, not only my dick, but my body in anticipation. She was going to be mine in more ways than just my mind. Her body would be mine, and soon, if not immediately, her heart also.

I opened the door and let her step in first. I came up behind her, my hands on her upper arms as she took it all in. Her head moved to the right where the walk-in closet was. To the bedside table where a picture of Simone sat. Which was when she took my hand off her arm and brought it around to kiss it. She was telling me it was okay to remember. It was okay to keep Simone alive in memory. Her head then moved left where the window sat, then to the wall next to it where the outside camera monitors were lined on a computer table. They flashed from one corner of the property to another.

"You weren't lying about keeping us safe," she murmured.

"Shit no. Most important people in this house. Do anything to keep them safe." Turning her in my arms and taking her face in my hands, I said, "Need you to know, from this night on, you sleep in here with me, where you've always belonged. You good with that?"

"Yes," she whispered.

My eyes ran over her face, taking it all in. Her blonde, sexy hair, her pale, warm blue eyes, her heart-shaped face, and her fuckable, kissable lips. Everything about her made me hard; her body, her voice, her whispers drove my cock crazy.

"Can't hold back, Mena. Need you. Now get naked and on the bed. I wanna watch you strip, watch you lie on the bed, spreading your legs, offering me your pussy."

With my hands still on her, I felt her whole body shiver, and I loved it. I knew her pussy would be wet already. Licking her lips, she stepped back. I let my hands drop from her even when they wanted to reach out to her. She stepped back again and slowly slid her tee up her stomach, over her breasts, which were covered in black lace, and threw it off her arms to the floor.

Her smile was shy. Her heart would be beating like crazy, like mine was in anticipation, but she continued. The little tease undid the button on her shorts in a leisurely pace. My eyes narrowed; hers smiled.

"Woman," I said in a warning tone. My heart was going crazy behind my chest. Having my eyes on *all* of her skin was something I'd been wanting for a hell of a long time. My dick jerked behind my jeans. A giggle left her lips as she unzipped her shorts and wiggled them over her hips and down her legs, kicking them off to the side.

Fuck. *Beautiful.*

My sunshine then reached behind her and unhooked her bra, dropping it to the floor.

As she watched me watch her, I glided my hand over my hard-on behind my jeans. I had to touch my hard cock. My gaze found her perfect breasts, and I focused on them, desperate to touch them. Her eyes followed my movement, her gaze dipping to a smouldering heat. She wanted what I was touching.

Her eyes flared, her mouth opened in a soft gasp before she picked up her pace. She removed her panties quickly and lay back on the bed, moving into the middle.

In a soft, lust-filled voice, she admitted, "I've never felt this need for someone before, Kalen. Just having you watch me with such intensity in your eyes makes me crazy. Makes me feel confident." When she'd finished her confession, she bent her knees, her feet going to the bed. Then she spread her legs wide for my eyes to feast upon her pussy. Heat filled her cheeks and ran quickly down her chest. From where I stood, I could see she was slick with need. My woman was aching, and I was about to settle it for her, while enjoying it greatly in doing so.

"Touch it," I demanded. She ran her fingers around her nipple and then down until they dipped into her hole. She arched and moaned. "Lick your fingers, Mena. Taste yourself." She met my gaze as she removed her fingers and slid them between her lips where she licked and sucked them.

Fuck. I was about to blow my load in my jeans.

"Kalen," she whispered huskily. "I need you."

"What do you need?" I removed my tee from my body. Her eyes fucked me over. Her small curve to her lips told me she liked my ink.

"You. I need you to fuck me."

"With goddamn pleasure." I kicked off my jeans and boxers. She smiled as I stalked towards her. "You're fucking beautiful."

"So are you." Her hands ran over her stomach, her tits, her mound.

Palming my cock, I stood beside the bed and asked, "This what you want?"

"Yes," she growled in her cute little voice. Reaching into the bedside table, I grabbed a condom out, tore the packet with my teeth, and rolled it on. She was expecting me to just take her. But I wasn't. I needed another taste of my woman's pussy.

With my knees to the bed, my hands went to her thighs, and I held them down as I lowered my upper body between her legs.

"Oh, God," she moaned even before I had my mouth on her pussy.

At the first touch of my tongue, her legs tried to come up around my head, but I held them down. I loved my pussy spread wide for me, so I could do what I wanted to do. My tongue dipped into her hole. She cried out. I slid it up circling her clit. She tasted even sweeter from the small dip I'd had at the club.

But, fuck me, I was close to coming.

Her hand threaded into my hair, and I fuckin' growled as she pushed my head down harder. I sucked her clit in and bit down gently. My woman was greedy. My dick twitched from her show of losing her shy self.

"Holy motherfucking...!" she cried out.

There was no way I was blowing without being in her. Before I could, I moved up her body, kissing every part I could and then met her greedy mouth with mine. She licked and sucked her own juices off me and shit, my eyes hooded. I licked my lips as desire tickled down my spine, drawing my balls up tight.

When I thrust my dick hard into her tight, drenched pussy, she ground her head back into the bed and screamed, "Kalen. Fuck yes. Yes. Fuck me."

Christ. I was a goner.

Gripping her hair, I demanded, "Eyes, Mena. Now." She opened them. A purr fell from her lips before I said, "You feel me? My cock deep inside of you? This is my pussy, sunshine. Fuckin' mine." She managed a nod just as her walls tightened around my cock. "Jesus. Yes. Milk my cock. Milk it."

She took my face in her hands and kissed me hard while I grunted through my load shooting out into the condom.

Slowing my thrusts, I got to my hands above her and looked down at my woman. Dipping my gaze lower, I watched my still hard cock slide in and out of her tight snatch.

"Fuckin' perfect." My words came out on a growl. "Hope you don't mind having minimal sleep."

She smiled up at me and said, "Not one bit."

MENA

A cheery voice woke me from my sleep. I stretched and strained my ears to hear what was being said.

"Thought I'd pop in to see my grandbaby. Where's Mena? She's usually up and in the kitchen by now," Judy said, her voice easily travelling down the hallway. Sitting immediately, I gripped the blanket to my naked chest.

Judy was back.

Judy was back, and I was in her son's bed.

Oh, my God.

"Mum," Kalen shot out harshly.

"What? I'm just going out to her room to see if she's awake yet. You and Koda aren't the only ones I've missed."

"Mum." Kalen ground the words out.

"Yes, son? Spit it out."

"Mena's not in her room."

"What did you do?" she barked. "Did you yell at her again, and she's run off? I swear I will take you over my knee and tan your arse, no matter the age you are. She is the best thing that has happened to you in a long time. If you don't see that, then you're looking out of your arse, and you'll have no hope in your future."

"Fucking hell." I heard Kalen groan. "She's in my bed."

My breath caught in my throat. The room fell silent.

Even Koda's chattering was gone. That was until an excited squeal spilled into the house.

"Holy shit. Holy shit!" Judy cheered. "I'm so proud of you, my son. This is the best news you could ever bring me, well, besides having knocked her up. But I'll let you slide on that one."

"What are you doing?" Kalen sounded exasperated.

"Taking Koda for a while. Get back in there with Mena, and you never know, you could tell me soon I'll have more grandchildren on the way."

My body flopped back on the bed, my hand covering my mouth to hide my laughter. Judy was amazing. I'd worried she'd think I was only after her son for his money or something ridiculous along those lines, but I didn't have to worry. I knew she'd seen what I'd been hiding for some time: my affection for Kalen Brooks.

THREE WEEKS LATER

MENA

When I got back from the store, I found Judy sitting on the couch reading a book to Koda.

"Hi." I smiled. "Where's Kalen?"

"Getting ready."

Stopping, I asked, "For what?"

"Dinner. He's taking you out, and I'm taking Koda home with me for the night." She grinned like a fool. I'd been right; Judy was more than pleased Kalen had gotten his act together and claimed me as his woman. It was something she'd told me many times.

My stomach dipped delightfully in excitement. Over the past few weeks, we hadn't had time to go on an official date night. Not that it bothered me so much. We spent all of our free time enjoying each other's company.

My head snapped to the hall when I heard Kalen's heavy footfalls approach. He was dressed in dark jeans, a tee, and his club's cut.

Grinning, I asked, "We're going on the bike?"

Kalen winked. "Yeah, sunshine. Dump that shit and go get on some jeans."

Looking down at my dress, I glanced up at Judy and whispered in a thrilled voice, "We're going on the bike."

She laughed. "Put your bags on the counter. I'll unpack for you before I head out with this little man."

Rushing the bags into the kitchen, I then raced back into the living room, down the hall and straight into Kalen's closet, our closest. All my clothes were among his. I had a bedside table with my panties and bras in it, on *my* side of the bed. Emotions had overwhelmed me the day he'd moved me in, and I ended up bursting into tears. Kalen, thank God, thought it was cute.

Dressed in jeans, an awesome biker babe tee, which Low had bought me—I'd found the parcel sitting in the letterbox a few days ago—and my own girly biker boots on my feet, I made my way down the hall with a giddy smile on my face.

Kalen grinned when he saw me, stood from the couch, and asked, "Ready?"

"Heck yes." After a kiss to Judy and Koda's cheeks, I took Kalen's hand and we headed to his Harley already sitting out front waiting for us. Since I'd been moved into the house, Kalen moved his Harley back into the shed, which he was glad to do. It was one of his babies after all.

I loved watching Kalen straddling his ride. It was when he turned into Dive. He kicked her to life, looked at me and winked before sliding his mirrored sunglasses over his eyes. Even though it was late, the sun was still setting. His chin lifted to me, gesturing for me to hop on. A spasm hit my clit. He looked like he belonged on his Harley. Warmth filled me. I was happy he'd found this part of himself. He'd found his family, a place he belonged, and now I was a part of it as well.

It was something special.

Climbing on the back, I placed my new helmet on and wound my arms around his middle and that time, there was no hesitation in bringing my body flush against his. His hand rubbed against my hand at his waist before it went back to the handle bar and we took off.

When he drove out of Halls Gap and took a scenic tour into the mountains, pleasure swept throughout my body. Being close to him, on his bike with the wind, and the feel between my legs from the bike's power was what I wanted more than food.

Free to think, my mind wandered to the previous night. Kalen had sat on the couch with his son on his knee when I'd walked into the room. He was showing Koda some pictures of Simone and talking about her. Telling him she was his mum. Tears filled my eyes when Koda looked up to Kalen and said, "Mum." Kalen had sensed my presence when I'd first entered. He seemed to be always in tune with me. At Koda's word, he'd looked over at me and smiled.

Practically skipping across the floor, I'd sat beside my guys and said, "Yes, Koda. That's your mum. Isn't she pretty?" Kalen wound his arm around my shoulders and kissed my temple. I sat there along with Koda and listened to the stories my man shared about Simone.

It was a moment in life, actually one of many, I would always remember and love.

We rode for two hours, but it only seemed like half an hour before we were pulling into the restaurant car park.

I was already off the bike and removing my helmet when Kalen came up behind me, his hands moving to my waist. "Fuckin' love that you enjoy riding as much as I do."

Placing the helmet on the seat, I turned in his arms and asked, "One day, when Koda is older and in school, could we take off for the whole day? Just stopping to eat and refuel?"

His eyes lowered in desire. "Fuck waiting. We'll do it soon. Mum will have Koda."

Smiling, I whispered against his lips, "Yay." Then I kissed him, wrapping my arms around his neck.

Pulling back, he said in a low voice, "Shit, we'd better eat so I can get you home to bed." He smirked at my blush, running the back of his hand over my cheek. "Fuckin' love it."

We walked into the restaurant and waited to be seated. I saw a waitress coming our way with a smile lighting her face once she spotted Kalen. Rolling my eyes, I curled my body around my man's and offered her a friendly smile. Kalen couldn't help he was so good-looking. Still, I wanted her to know he belonged to someone, and that there were no hard feelings. She could look, admire even, but not touch. Her smile faltered as Kalen threw his head back and roared with laughter.

His hand ran over my arse as the waitress took us to an available table. Was I shy about it being in public? No, I owned it.

She asked for our drink orders, which we gave, and then she left with a huff when Kalen wouldn't even look at her.

"I want more kids," he stated just as I picked up the

menu, only to have it fall from my fingers, bang on the table and drop to the floor.

"Sorry?" I was sure I'd heard him wrong.

"First, need you on the pill for a bit. Want my time with you and Koda before I knock you up, and I wanna be able to come inside you and still be protected until we decide it's time to have more trouble runnin' around."

My mouth opened, and my heart did a ballet dance in my chest. I wanted to bring my hand up to still my heart, but I was too busy clenching and unclenching them in my lap from the way his words had stolen everything from me, yet warmed me at the same time.

Noise to the side caused me to jump. The waitress had reappeared placing our drinks on the table. Beer for Kalen and a lemon lime and bitters for me.

"Ready to order?" she asked.

"I'll have the steak and chips. Mena?" He smirked. He'd completely caught me off guard, and he loved it.

"Um," I started. "The, ah, f-fish please."

"Sure," she said and then left.

"Kalen," I whispered. "You want kids with me, but first, you want me on the pill before we decide to have them…? Did I get that right or was I dreaming?"

He chuckled. "Got it right in one, sunshine. Except you're missing the part where I can't wait to go ungloved inside of you." Wiggling in my seat, he laughed again. "See you're down with that. Good." Leaning forward, he added, "Grateful you came into my life, Mena. Grateful my dick moves at the start didn't scare you off. Most of all, I'm fuckin' grateful you filled my heart with love once again."

"Kalen," I mumbled. My bottom lip trembled. Tears stung my eyes. A need to be close to him hit me. Not caring with the people around us, I pushed my chair back and stood. His smile told me he knew what I was doing. His own chair slid back, and I moved around and sat sideways in his lap. My face hit the crook of his neck and shoulder. "I love you. I really do."

A grunt. "Fuckin' love you, sunshine."

Lifting my head, I met his gaze with a serious one. "But I need you to know, it's been on my mind for a while and I-I need to get it out because I worry… with my debt, my money situation. I-I don't want you to think I'm only with you for it to be easier on me. You and Koda are my world—"

"Enough," he said with an honest to God growl. "Never would I think it. We'll take care of shit together. Have no worries about what I think, Mena. Your heart it pure gold. I know it."

Nodding, I whispered, "Okay."

"Okay." He smiled. "Together, everything will work out."

"Together." I smiled and then kissed him right there in front of anyone who wanted to watch.

LATER THAT NIGHT, Kalen had just walked naked from the bathroom into the bedroom. I was already stripped bare and lying on the bed waiting for him. His smirk was cocky as he climbed up my body. His knees went to the side of my head, and in a voice that sent a quiver to my clit, he ordered, "Suck me."

He knew I loved taking his cock in my mouth as much as he liked going down on me, but that night, I was going to switch it up a bit. Opening my mouth, he slid his cock in slowly and then back out again.

"Love your pussy, but love your mouth just as much," he said gliding himself into my mouth again. A groan escaped his lips as I swirled my tongue around the tip when he pulled back out.

While he was busy with my mouth, my hand went under the sheet where I stored some lube. I clicked the lid open and squirted some on my fingers. His head was thrown back as he fucked my face, his hips sinking in and out faster. I placed my hands to his arse; something I know he liked was when I helped his hips with my hands to fuck my face harder.

Slowly, testing the waters, I ran my finger up his crack. When he didn't shift away, I slid in a lubed finger and added pressure to his hole. He stilled, his cock pulled from my mouth.

His head dipped down, and he clipped out harshly, "What the fuck are you doing?"

"Do you trust me?" I asked.

"I ain't into that." He went to move, but I grabbed his legs, stopping him.

"Are you scared?"

"What the fuck, woman?" He scoffed. "No."

"Please, let me. If you don't like it, I'll stop, but I know, I've read up on it, and I know you'll come harder this way."

His lips twitched. "You've read about this shit?"

"Yes. I want to pleasure you—"

He groaned. "You already fuckin' pleasure me."

"But this will be different and… and it turns me on."

His eyes narrowed. "You're just saying that shit to get your way."

"Please?" I begged, kissing the tip of his cock. "Please?" A kiss to his thigh. "Please?" A kiss to his balls and then I sucked one into my mouth.

"Fuckin' hell." He sighed, and it turned into a grunt. "Keep sucking me off, and we'll see where it goes."

Yes! I rubbed my thighs together. I wasn't lying. Kalen giving me something I wanted in bed was an extra stage up in my horniness. I was soaked below, so wet I knew I was leaking out onto the sheets.

He slipped his cock into my mouth once again. He moaned low. My hands went back to his arse. He stiffened for a second until I twirled my tongue around his head and sucked hard. "Fuck," he growled and pumped harder into my mouth.

My finger was once again at his crack, and then I slid a finger in. It was still lubed, so I rubbed it against his entrance. When he thrust back from my mouth, I inserted the tip.

"Jesus, Mena," he gritted out. Gently, I glided my finger in and out, only to the knuckle so he could get used to it. "What are you doing to me?" He grunted when he pushed back on my finger, and it went all the way in. He swore and groaned loudly when I touched his prostate. "Fuck. Fucking hell."

His hands went from the headboard to the pillow, and he looked down at me, eyes hot and heavy with desire. As he fucked my face, I finger fucked his arse, hitting his spot over and over, and I knew, by his clenched jaw, by the sweat pooling over his body and his hooded eyes, he loved every second of it.

"Christ," he snarled. "Fuck, yes. Do it, harder. Jesus. Yes. Fuck. God, I-I'm gonna come." Twisting my finger, he growled out a grunted groan as I rubbed my finger over his inside. His cum shot into my mouth; luckily I loved it. I drank it down because it kept coming and coming.

Slipping my finger out of him, he shifted back to pull

his cock from my mouth. "Give me a second," he panted. "I feel drained."

I giggled. "So you'll let me do it again?" I asked.

He moved to sit behind my head. His brows rose and he asked, "You really liked it?"

Taking his hand in mine, I led it between my legs. His eyes widened. "Christ, you're soaked. Jesus, it's leaking outta you."

"I loved doing that to you."

"If that's the case, yeah, sunshine, you can do whatever you want to me. But now, get in the fuckin' shower. I'm gonna eat all your juices while we get clean."

My body shivered. Then I did as I was told.

EPILOGUE

FOUR MONTHS LATER

DIVE

Happiness had touched my soul once again. When Simone died, I never thought I'd get it back. I certainly didn't expect Philomena McAdams to show up at my doorstep and change my world. It took us a long fucking time to get our shit sorted. Well, mostly it was me, but finally, she was mine, and I wasn't wasting time with this one.

Life *was* too short.

Simone was proof enough. Mena was mine, and she

was the best thing that could have stumbled into my dark world with her sunshine.

To make it understood, make her understand she was mine, I was about to put a ring on her finger, a ring my mum gave me, saying it was her grandmother's. A ring that meant something to her, so it meant something to me. When I'd mentioned I was asking Mena, Mum went crazy. I was surprised her neighbours didn't come running in to see what was wrong with her. She also mentioned Mena was special and having me back to the way I was, except less perverted, had proved how special my woman was.

While I waited for Mena to get back from reading Koda a story, I used the time to hunt through my closet for the stored ring. I was just coming back out of the closet when she walked in.

"Get your cute arse to bed, woman," I ordered and quickly slid my boxers off while placing the ring box under the bed.

"My man need some loving?"

"Shit, yeah he does, and he wants you to do all the work."

She scoffed and rolled her eyes. "Lazy arse."

With my knees to the bed, I reached out and tagged her around the waist, flipping her down to the bed. "You love taking control. Don't lie to me, sunshine," I said and leaned over her.

"I do. I really do." She smirked, and I knew she remembered the night she fucked my arse with her finger. Never in my life would I have expected to get off on something like that, but I did, and I fucking blew my load hard. I reckoned it was because it was my woman giving it to me. Mena reached up and patted my cheek. "As long as you don't take over."

Chuckling, I lay on my back and said, "Have at me, and I'll see what I can do."

Smiling, she climbed on top. Slowly, she leaned down and licked my nipple, then pulled back and blew on it. My fucking body shuddered. She giggled, loving the reaction she could pull from me. Mena trailed her lips up my chest, my neck, and fucking finally, she claimed my mouth with a searing wild kiss. Her hands gripped my hair and pulled. Loved it when she lost control. She ground her pussy down on my cock. My hands went to her waist, only she grabbed them, pulled back, and said. "Nuh-uh. No touching." She winked, and I groaned. She forced my hands above my head and then slid hers down to my sides where I flinched because it fucking tickled, causing her to giggle. She kept going down to my hips. Only then, she stood and dragged her boy-shorts down her legs, bearing her pussy for me.

"I'm going to sit on your face, Kalen, but if you touch me once, I'll move."

"Bitch," I growled. She threw her head back and

laughed. She knew, *fuckin' knew* how much I loved her pussy, but I loved touching her while she fucked my face just as much.

"Scoot down a bit," she ordered. I did. I'd do anything for her pussy on my mouth, and she also knew that.

Her knees came down each side of my head. She lowered further so her lips just touched my mouth. "Lower," I snarled. She laughed, only to stop when she glided her hands down my chest, stomach and then wrapped her hands around my cock.

I wanted to palm her arse and drag her pussy to my mouth, but I didn't. Instead, I lifted my head, just as she took my dick into her sweet mouth, and licked the seam. She mewed at the first lick. She loved her pussy being eaten. So much so, I lost her mouth on my cock, and she sat up, bringing her pussy down onto my mouth. My tongue parted her lips, and she ground back and forth on my mouth as my tongue tasted, drank, and fucked her pussy.

"Kalen," she whimpered. "Yes."

Her hand slapped to my chest while she rocked her entrance back and forth over my mouth. My growl into her pussy caused her to moan from the sensation.

Jesus, I'd do just about anything if she'd let me touch her.

Just from her juices I was about to blow.

She was close to coming. Her hips picked up, sliding

her pussy quickly up and down on my mouth. Her head was thrown back, and she was making noises in the back of her throat.

Ah, fuck it. I grabbed her hips and pulled her down harder, so my tongue went straight into her just as she cried out her orgasm.

While she kept coming, I flipped her off me, got between her legs, and slammed into her. She screamed her pleasure down my throat as I kissed her hard.

"Fuckin' amazin'," I snarled. "So good. Fuckin' love your pussy, sunshine. All mine." I mumbled as I pumped my cock hard into her. She lifted her hips to greet me thrust for thrust.

"Oh. Shit. Kalen."

It still brought a smile to my face every time she swore while I was fucking her because she never swore any other time.

"Look at me," I ordered.

She dipped her chin and opened her heated eyes. Smiling, she wrapped her legs around my waist and reached a hand up to cup my cheek.

"Feel you," she whispered and then moaned when her pussy tightened around my cock as she came.

"Look at me," I demanded. She was still coming but managed to open her eyes and meet my gaze just as I grunted through my cum shooting out, planting deep inside her. Just thinking about it, I wanted to have her again. My dick was still hard, and I was still rocking inside of her, but I needed to do something first before I took her again.

Staring down at her, I said, "Got my seed in you, got my sweat on you. Want my ring on your finger, sunshine. You'll be mine, yeah?"

"Yes, Kalen." She smiled up at me, tears shining in her eyes. Our kiss was tender, hot, and sweet.

Slipping my cock from her, I leaned down over the bed and grabbed the box. She quickly shifted up to a sitting position and leaned against the headboard. Tears sprung in her eyes once again, only that time, as I slid the ring on her finger, her tears fell.

After looking down at the ring, she glanced up at me. Her expression was bright. Even though tears shone in her eyes, her smile was wide and she giddily whispered, "It's beautiful." Fuck, she made me happy. Jesus, it felt like it wanted to burst out of me in song. Not that I'd let that happen.

Instead, I tagged her around the neck and pulled her close. She rested her head against my chest, and then I gruffly said, "I'm the luckiest man to have your beauty in my bed, in my arms, and for the rest of my life."

I'd just claimed my woman in every way, and I couldn't be fucking happier.

FIVE HOURS LATER

When the phone rang, I cursed it to hell. I goddamn loved my sleep, but most of all, I loved holding my woman while we slept. So anything to break me away from her would shit me up the wall. Anything except Koda.

Sitting up, I shifted my feet to the ground, and felt Mena's hand run down my back. "Yo," I barked into it.

"Brother," Dodge answered. His tone was off. It was quiet, and I knew right then something was going down.

"Talk," I demanded. Mena moved up to sit behind me, curling her arms around my waist. She was alert.

"Need you, man. Need you to come home. Nary's been taken. I'm ringing Stoke soon. I'll need you here for when he arrives. And Saxon, fuck, brother. Fuck," he hissed. "He's not good. We had to lock him down. Messages been sent out, all brothers on board. We'll need fuckin' everyone."

"Christ. Jesus Christ. Nary. I'm there, brother." I hung up and stood. My woman got up and wound her arms around me.

"Nary?"

"She's been taken, sunshine. I need to help."

She nodded. "Then let's get Koda and go home, Kalen. It was time anyway."

"It's time," I agreed. "You know I'll do anything to keep you and Koda safe?"

"I know, honey. I'll never be scared in any type of situation because I know I have my man to take care of me."

"Damn right."

"Love you, Kalen Brooks."

"Right back at you, soon-to-be Mrs Brooks."

And even though dread filled me for Nary, I still felt at peace. No longer would I feel down and out, not when I had my sunshine at my side.

CHAPTER ONE

NARY

At the age of twenty, some would think I would have known what I wanted with my life. I didn't. No, that wasn't right. I knew where I wanted my career to go at least. What my mind was up in the air about was my love life.

As I walked to my car, my thoughts wandered. It was only then I realised it was so late. The stars shone while the cool air held a scent of rain. I found myself glad my uni had enough lights around to spotlight the car park. I pulled my eyes down to my watch; I was late for my pizza date, and no doubt, Jerimiah would be worried. Especially when he found out I hadn't left the media room with a group of people like I'd told him I would. Regret formed low in my belly, churning it. I'd wanted time alone to work on my assignment, so it was my own stupid fault for lying and becoming paranoid someone was watching me.

Thinking of Jerimiah, a smile formed on my mouth and I couldn't help but picture the time I'd met him. He had been in my business class; it had been the only one we'd shared together, and throughout it, he'd kept glancing over at me. Of course I noticed out the corner of my eyes, who wouldn't, especially when the best-looking guy in there tried to catch my attention. As soon as I met his gaze, he'd smiled and waved. Then he'd actually blushed. I'd offered an attentive smile back and gazed back down to my work. It was the next class where I'd found the—usually free—seat next to me occupied by Jerimiah. My heart had skipped a beat and my stomach had started playing havoc, as if there was a stampede of tiny bulls running wild in there. As soon as I'd sat, he'd turned to me and introduced himself. From that day on, we'd become close, having coffee with each other, going to the movies, and spending hours studying together.

This was despite Jerimiah being a part of the Venom MC, a club that brought my family's MC club, the Hawks, nothing but trouble. I'd discovered about his membership two years earlier, but that hadn't stopped us forming a relationship.

It had been two weeks after Jerimiah and I had met and become friends—with a side of something else, something that warmed my belly—when I'd gone to the Hawks compound in search of either Josie or Low. I'd needed advice.

I open the front office door to the side mechanical business at the compound, only to find the office empty. With a frown, I walk to the door that opens into the garage. Stepping out, I see Muff, a biker brother to the Caroline Springs Hawks charter.

"Hey, Muff. Do you know if Low or Josie is here?"

"Nah, babe. I think Josie is at uni and Low's out with Dive somewhere."

"Nary," is bit out behind me. Straightaway, I know who it is. I know his voice, regardless of the tone, anywhere. Though with me, it's always growly, snappy, or short.

Turning, I face Saxon. He's the one man who takes my breath away, who stole my heart when I was sixteen, who is on my mind constantly. Even when he's a prick to me, my heart doesn't seem to care. Though my mind often tells me to forget about him.

"Saxon?"

"Office, now," he clips before he turns and steps back into the office.

Listening to my mind, which tells me to ignore his order

and get out of there, isn't an option, especially when my heart beats faster in his presence. It has me following him silently.

Moving through the door, I stop just on the other side to find Saxon already near the front entrance with his arms crossed over his chest scowling at me. "Dodge wants to see you in his office out back."

My head jerks back. Why couldn't he have told me that in front of Muff?

When I realise that's all he wants to say, my shoulders sag in defeat. He holds nothing in his heart for me, and I have to stop holding out hope for him. Looking to the floor, I nod, turn, and walk back into the garage. Anger has me slapping my feet on the concrete floor harder than usual as I stomp towards Dodge's office. Another question slips into my mind. Why does Dodge want to see me in his office?

Ignoring it, I come to the door and swing it open. My eyes widen when I notice it isn't only Dodge in there, but other members fill the space and the room is thick with tension.

"Nary?" Dodge asks.

"Oh, um...." My eyes shift around the room, and a gasp falls from my lips. "You, you're... no," I whisper before turning and running back down the hall. Seeing Jerimiah standing in there, behind a man who looks like him wearing a Venom MC vest, slices hurt through me. Even in the two weeks I knew him, he could have said something.

He hadn't.

I bolt through the garage, as someone calls out to me, but I ignore him and keep running, right outside. My chest hurts with the breath I try to gulp in from the shock and adrenaline pounding through me. With fast movements, I make it to my car and unlock it. However, before I get in, I look back to the garage once, and I wish I hadn't.

Standing outside, leaning against the brick wall is Saxon and on his handsome face is a smirk.

That day I finally realised Saxon and I would never be anything to each other.

The knowledge had settled deep within my lower abdomen, causing it to churn with a hollowed sadness.

I'd always hoped, always believed he would have eventually seen what we could have been one day.

He'd known who I would see in the room that day. And he'd been happy my heart had hurt at the betrayal that had sliced through me from Jerimiah keeping something from me.

The whole scene had angered me, and yet my heart still cared for Saxon.

Honestly, I had started to consider my heart as a second person because my mind was on a different path to what my heart had felt. My mind was sick of my unrequited love for Saxon. Rejection stung. It wanted to move on, and it could with a guy like Jerimiah. Which was why I had been officially dating Jerimiah for the last four months. He'd come to my apartment two years ago, after that night I'd discovered he was a part of Venom and explained his whole situation of having a controlling father. He didn't want to be with Venom, and he'd told me as soon as he could, he'd make the move to leave. From the time I'd already spent with him, I'd felt as though I could trust him, and his words. So I continued being his friend, until twenty months later when he'd kissed me one night. The touch of his lips had sent my body into a wave of desire.

He was sweet, caring, rough, and just what I'd needed.

He showed me I was worth something. His time and feelings.

Even a part of my heart warmed to the idea of letting it all go to Jerimiah. He treated me right. He didn't ignore me or look at me with disgust in his eyes. He didn't think I was being a stupid girl with a small crush.

Saxon had been hurtful on so many occasions, so why couldn't I let my whole heart fall for Jerimiah and let go of what I tried to cling to for Saxon? I should hate him. He wanted me to. He tried to get me to in so many ways.

Sighing, I unlocked my car door and tried to rid my thoughts of Saxon. Besides, I was heading home to meet with Jerimiah for a study date, which would probably end up in a make-out session. My boyfriend was sweet and very thoughtful. He was hot, as in smoking, and his smile always brought one of my own to my mouth.

"Nary." My name was yelled from across the yard. Looking up, I spotted Josie standing near the building, under the light, smiling wide and waving. I giggled to myself. Jerimiah had probably called her or one of her guys to make sure I made it to my car safely. Jerimiah had wanted to stay back with me, but I'd told him not to because I was safe at the always-bustling university, no matter the time of the day or night.

Everyone who had a connection to the Hawks MC was more cautious because of Baxter Davis. He had it out for all members of Hawks and wanted us to pay in one way or another. I wasn't sure why he had a vendetta against my Hawks family, but it was there, and until someone put a stop to him, we all had to be careful, making sure no one was alone.

Still, I thought no one would be stupid enough to try anything at the university. As I looked to Josie and offered a smile and wave back, I noticed all the people walking or rushing around, either coming from the cafeteria or going out for the night. Just behind Josie, my eyes landed on Billy. He somehow saw my gaze and offered me a chin lift. What could have helped his view of me was the street lamp I'd purposefully parked under. My friend was one lucky woman having two men at her back. Two men who loved her so deeply, they were willing to share. She deserved happiness.

"I'll see you tomorrow," I yelled with another wave. I wanted to get in the car so I could get to my place and Jerimiah. My stomach growled at the thought of the delicious pizza. It also flipped at the thought of the man who would be waiting for me. Things were progressing well with Jerimiah and myself. We hadn't moved to the final stage of the relationship. Something was holding me back from sleeping with him. Yet, we still fooled around and a thrill bubbled up inside me each time, even when the learning process was sometimes embarrassing. Still, Jerimiah was patient, and he enjoyed teaching as much as I loved experiencing.

As I threw my bag across to the passenger seat and I was about to slide in myself, my name was screeched across the area. My gaze rose to see Josie running for me. Billy was on her heels and about to take over her as he reached into the back of his jeans and pulled a gun, pointed right at me.

My eyes widened. A scream built in my throat, but it never erupted from my mouth because a hand covered it.

My eyes connected with Josie's. Fear. All I could see was fear. My stomach dropped in panic. My body trembled in terror. People roared in alarm as a shot was fired. My captor, a man, something I could tell from the large body behind me, cursed as I was roughly pulled down to the ground. A car's engine revved high near us. I craned my neck back to try to get my mouth free. I couldn't. Still, I screamed behind it. I kicked, grabbed hold of the arm holding me around the waist, and ripped into the skin with my fingernails. He swore and jolted me back and forth hard against him. "Stop," he warned.

Why wasn't anyone doing anything?

I heard more screams around me. People rushing our way. People running away. Another shot was fired. It pinged off the roof of the car just before I was pulled up and shoved inside. I yelled, kicking out at the man trying to get in after me. He grabbed my leg and bent it in a way that I cried out in pain.

He shoved harder, and I scooted back and tried the other door. Even though the lock wasn't in place, the door wouldn't open. I growled in frustration at my attempt. I banged my fists against the glass. I screamed, cried, while tears ran freely down my cheeks.

Nothing worked.

No one helped me in time.

The car sped away with me inside it.

Frantically, I climbed to my knees. My hands went to the back window. Billy was there, standing in the middle of the road, lights shinning down on him. I saw the gun pointed right at us. Though he didn't fire, no doubt worried it would hit me. His face crumpled in rage before he threw his hands up in the air and screamed. Josie ran onto the road and started for the car. I could no longer see her face clearly through my own tears and the darkness surrounding us, but I knew she would be feeling everything I was.

Pure horror.

My hair was grasped and my head tugged back. The man sitting next to me moved his face close to mine. He was in his early thirties, with a shaved head, a beard, and blue eyes that told me I was not in a nightmare. I was living one, and he would be happy to deliver some pain.

"Sit the fuck down," he bit out. "You'd better behave. I don't have to deliver you fully intact," he commented before he harshly pushed me back to my bottom in the corner of the car.

"D-do you know who I am?" I asked on a whisper. Glancing to the man in the front driving the car, who drove like a crazy person, I saw his gaze flick to me. Hard, dark green eyes stared back for a second before they went back to the road.

"Nope, and I don't give a fuck. I was told to keep an eye on you, grab you when I could, so I did." He eyed me up and down my body, a smirk spread across his face. "Boss Baxter knows when a good thing would pay and, honey, people will wanna pay big bucks for you." He studied my face and abruptly asked, "How'd you get the scar?"

"A gun shot."

"What happened to the person who gave it to you?"

"He's dead. Just like you will be if you don't let me go. My family will do anything to get me back."

He scoffed. "Yeah? And who's your family?"

Sitting up, I jutted my chin out in fake bravado and replied, "The Hawks MC."

His gaze went to the driver's in the rear-view mirror. The driver shrugged and my captor turned back to me. "Like I said, don't give a fuck. You'll be outta my hair and in my boss' soon enough, and then it becomes his problem."

Licking my dry lips, I laughed without humour. "If you think so. But I can tell you now, the men of Hawks harm everyone involved when taking what belongs to them. Everyone."

His jaw clenched. He shifted forward and pulled something from his back pocket. "You're annoying me. Time to go bye-bye." His arm shot out and I looked down as a taser was placed against my stomach. With one shock, I was out.

ACKNOWLEDGEMENTS

Craig and our two monsters, thank you for your help in cleaning, cooking, and keeping me going when times get busy.

Lindsey Lawson, for your help right from the start.

Becky and her team at Hot Tree Editing and Donna at Hot Tree Promotions, thank you for all your hard work with *Down and Out.*

Justine Littleton, for telling me how it is in her unique way.

TL Smith, I freaking cherish the friendship we have, and I'm glad I have you to travel with.

Julie King and Justine Littleton, for the title *Down and Out.*

Charlene Brotherston, for suggesting Julian and Mattie's child's name!

ALSO BY LILA ROSE

Hawks MC: Ballarat Charter

Holding Out (FREE) Zara and Talon

Climbing Out: Griz and Deanna

Finding Out (novella) Killer and Ivy

Black Out: Blue and Clarinda

No Way Out: Stoke and Malinda

Coming Out (novella) Mattie and Julia

Hawks MC: Caroline Springs Charter

The Secret's Out: Pick, Billy and Josie

Hiding Out: Dodge and Willow

Down and Out: Dive and Mena

Living Without: Vicious and Nary

Walkout (novella) Dallas and Melissa

Hear Me Out: Beast and Knife

Breakout (novella) Handle and Della

Fallout: Fang and Poppy

Standalones related to the Hawks MC

Out of the Blue (Lan, Easton, and Parker's story)

Out Gamed (novella) (Nancy and Gamer's story)

Outplayed (novella) (Violet and Travis's story)

Romantic comedies

Making Changes

Making Sense

Fumbled Love

Trinity Love Series

Left to Chance

Love of Liberty (novella)

Paranormal

Death (with Justine Littleton)

In The Dark

CONNECT WITH LILA ROSE

Webpage: www.lilarosebooks.com

Facebook: http://bit.ly/2du0taO

Instagram: www.instagram.com/lilarose78/

Goodreads:

www.goodreads.com/author/show/7236200.Lila_Rose

www.ingramcontent.com/pod-product-compliance
Lightning Source LLC
Chambersburg PA
CBHW071535110726

47908CB00007B/1897

Advance Praise for *Echo Year*

"In this well-crafted literary novel, the author captures the myriad nuances of a midlife crisis and brings to life an idyllic village in the French Midi only to haunt it with dark forces. The perfect chateau proves no refuge for protagonist David Crown. Amid a hail of firebombs and truffles, his world comes tumbling down."

David Liss

Praise for *Hotel Noir*

"A noirish combination of F. Scott Fitzgerald and early P. D. James on steroids, as told by a narrator who knows how to weave a web and pull you in without your realizing that you are caught. An intriguing literary crime novel filled with wonderfully zany characters Agatha Christie would have killed for."

Sam Millar, *NY Journal of Books*